Stroke of Midnight

Also from Lara Adrian

Midnight Breed Series

A Touch of Midnight (prequel novella FREE eBook)
Kiss of Midnight
Kiss of Crimson
Midnight Awakening
Midnight Rising
Veil of Midnight
Ashes of Midnight
Shades of Midnight
Taken by Midnight
Deeper Than Midnight
A Taste of Midnight (ebook novella)
Darker After Midnight
The Midnight Breed Series Companion
Edge of Dawn
Marked by Midnight (novella)
Crave the Night
Tempted by Midnight (novella)
Bound to Darkness
Stroke of Midnight
...*and more to come!*

Masters of Seduction Series

Merciless: House of Gravori
Priceless: House of Ebarron

Phoenix Code Series

Cut and Run (Books 1 & 2)
Hide and Seek (Books 3 & 4)

Historical Romances

Dragon Chalice Series
Heart of the Hunter (FREE eBook)
Heart of the Flame
Heart of the Dove
Dragon Chalice Boxed Set

Warrior Trilogy
White Lion's Lady (FREE eBook)
Black Lion's Bride
Lady of Valor
Warrior Trilogy Boxed Set

Standalone Titles
Lord of Vengeance

Stroke of Midnight

A Midnight Breed Novella

By Lara Adrian

1001 Dark Nights

EVIL EYE
CONCEPTS

Stroke of Midnight
A Midnight Breed Novella
By Lara Adrian

1001 Dark Nights
Copyright 2015 Lara Adrian, LLC
ISBN: 978-1-940887-32-6

Foreword: Copyright 2014 M. J. Rose
Published by Evil Eye Concepts, Incorporated

Acknowledgments

I am thrilled to be part of the 1001 Dark Nights collection for a second time with this novella in my Midnight Breed vampire romance series. My thanks to the awesome and endlessly creative Liz Berry, MJ Rose, Jillian Stein, and everyone else working behind the scenes at Evil Eye Concepts to make the project a success. Big hugs to my fellow 1001 Dark Nights authors as well. Every year, the lineup gets more impressive and the depth of talent more amazing. I'm grateful for your support and honored to call so many of you my friends.

And I have to send out lots of love and heartfelt thanks to my readers. I can't tell you what it means to me that you continue to embrace my characters and my work. I hope you have fun reading this new Midnight Breed adventure, and I hope you enjoy all the rest still to come!

With love,

Lara Adrian

Sign up for the 1001 Dark Nights Newsletter
and be entered to win a Tiffany Key necklace.

There's a contest every month!

Go to www.1001DarkNights.com to subscribe.

As a bonus, all subscribers will receive a free
1001 Dark Nights story
The First Night
by Lexi Blake & M.J. Rose

One Thousand and One Dark Nights

Once upon a time, in the future…

*I was a student fascinated with stories and learning.
I studied philosophy, poetry, history, the occult, and
the art and science of love and magic. I had a vast
library at my father's home and collected thousands
of volumes of fantastic tales.*

*I learned all about ancient races and bygone
times. About myths and legends and dreams of all
people through the millennium. And the more I read
the stronger my imagination grew until I discovered
that I was able to travel into the stories… to actually
become part of them.*

*I wish I could say that I listened to my teacher
and respected my gift, as I ought to have. If I had, I
would not be telling you this tale now.
But I was foolhardy and confused, showing off
with bravery.*

*One afternoon, curious about the myth of the
Arabian Nights, I traveled back to ancient Persia to
see for myself if it was true that every day Shahryar
(Persian: شهریار, "king") married a new virgin, and then
sent yesterday's wife to be beheaded. It was written
and I had read, that by the time he met Scheherazade,
the vizier's daughter, he'd killed one thousand
women.*

*Something went wrong with my efforts. I arrived
in the midst of the story and somehow exchanged
places with Scheherazade — a phenomena that had
never occurred before and that still to this day, I
cannot explain.*

Now I am trapped in that ancient past. I have taken on Scheherazade's life and the only way I can protect myself and stay alive is to do what she did to protect herself and stay alive.

Every night the King calls for me and listens as I spin tales. And when the evening ends and dawn breaks, I stop at a point that leaves him breathless and yearning for more. And so the King spares my life for one more day, so that he might hear the rest of my dark tale.

As soon as I finish a story... I begin a new one... like the one that you, dear reader, have before you now.

CHAPTER 1

Screams shot up from one of the many narrow, cobbled alleyways in the heart of Rome's quaint old Trastevere ward. The shrieks of mortal terror pierced the night as effectively as a blade.

Or, rather, a pair of razor-sharp fangs.

Like the ones on the gang of lethal predators who'd shredded the throat of a human civilian in a dance club across the city only minutes ago.

Shit. Jehan swung an urgent look over his shoulder to the two other Breed warriors currently on foot behind him. "They're getting away."

He and his teammates from the Order's Rome command center had been in pursuit of the four blood-thirsty Rogues since their patrol had been alerted to the killing at the club. They had contained the situation before any of the other humans had realized what was going on, but their mission wouldn't be over until they ashed the feral members of their own race.

"Split up," he told his men. "Damn it, we can't lose them! Close in from all sides."

His comrade and good friend, Savage, grinned and gave a nod of his blond head before veering right to take one of the other winding alleys on Jehan's command. The other warrior, a hulking, shaved-head menace called Trygg, made no acknowledgment to his team leader before vanishing into the darkness like a wraith to carry out the order.

Jehan sped like an arrow through the tight artery of the ancient street ahead of him, dodging slow-moving compact cars and taxis who were getting nowhere fast in the district that was clogged with tourists and club-hoppers even as the hour crept close to midnight.

The public out and about tonight was a mix of human and Breed civilians, something that would have been unheard of just twenty years ago, before the Breed's existence had been revealed to mankind.

Now, in cities around the world, the two populations lived together openly. They worked together. Governed together. But their hard-won peace was fragile. All it might take was one horrific killing—like the one earlier tonight—to set off a global panic.

While every Breed warrior of the Order had pledged his blood and breath to prevent that from happening, others among mankind and the Breed were secretly—and not-so-secretly—instigating war.

Tonight's Rogue attack had the stamp of conspiracy all over it. And it wasn't the first. During the past few nights there had been a handful of others, in Rome and elsewhere in Europe. While it wasn't unusual for one of Jehan's kind to become irreversibly addicted to blood, the spate of recent slayings in all-too-public places by Rogues torqued up on some kind of Bloodlust-inducing narcotic had fingers pointing to the terror group called Opus Nostrum.

Just a few days ago, the Order had scored a staggering hit on Opus, taking out its newest leader, who'd been headquartered in Ireland. The cabal was hobbled for now, but its hidden members were many and their machinations seemed to know no bounds. They and all who served them had to be stopped, or the consequences were certain to be catastrophic.

Jehan was a blur of motion as he leapt over the hood of a standing taxi to vault himself up onto the tiled rooftops above the thick congestion on the streets.

His heavy black patrol boots made no sound as he traveled with preternatural stealth and speed over the uneven terrain of the buildings. He jumped from one rooftop to the next, following his instincts—and the trace, metallic scent of fresh blood that floated up on the night breeze as the Rogue attempted to escape his pursuers.

He lived for this kind of action. The adrenaline rush. The thrill of the chase. The conviction that came from doing something with real purpose, something that would have true and lasting impact on his world.

A far cry from the posh wealth and useless decadence he'd been born into with his family in Morocco.

That old life was still trying to call him back, even though he hadn't stepped foot on his homeland's soil for more than a decade.

It had been twelve months and a day since he'd received the message from his father. Jehan knew what that meant, and he couldn't pretend he hadn't heard every tick of the damned countdown clock in the time since.

With a growl, he pushed aside reminders of the obligation he'd been pointedly ignoring. Right now, his focus was better spent on the more urgent mission in front of him.

Down below in a twisting alleyway, Jehan spied one of the fleeing Rogues. Fingers gripping the handle of one of his titanium blades, he drew the weapon and let it fly. Direct hit. The dagger nailed the Rogue in the center of his spine, dropping him in his tracks.

Ordinarily, it took more than that to disable one of the Breed, but the titanium was toxic to vampires who'd gone Rogue, and as corrosive as acid to their diseased bodies. In minutes or less, the corpse would be nothing but ashes in the street.

Jehan didn't wait to see the disintegration happen. As he continued his dash across the rooftops, he spotted Trygg gaining ground on one of the remaining Rogues. The big warrior took the escaping vampire down in a flash of movement. The Rogue howled, then abruptly fell silent when Trygg severed its head with a slice of his blade.

Two down. Two to go.

Make that one left to go. Jehan's acute hearing picked up sounds of a brief struggle as Savage caught up to his quarry on a different stretch of cobblestones and delivered a killing strike of titanium.

Jehan leapt to another roof, racing deeper into the ancient district of the city. His battle instincts heightened as he homed in on the last of the fleeing Rogues. The vampire made a crucial mistake, turning into an alleyway with no exit. A literal dead end.

Jehan sailed off the edge of the rooftop and dropped to the cobbled street behind the Rogue, cutting off any hope of his escape. An instant later, Savage emerged from out of the shadows, just as the feral vampire spun around and realized he had nowhere left to run.

The big male faced the two Order warriors. His fangs dripped with blood and sticky saliva. His transformed eyes glowed bright amber, the pupils fixed and narrowed to thin vertical slits in the center of all that fiery light. His jaw hung open as he roared, insane with Bloodlust and ready to attack.

Jehan didn't allow him the chance.

He threw his dagger without mercy or warning. The titanium blade glinted in the moonlight as the weapon sliced through the distance and struck its mark, burying to the hilt in the center of the Rogue's chest.

The vampire roared in agony, then collapsed in a heap on the cobbles as the poisonous metal began to devour him.

When the process had finished, Jehan strode over to retrieve his weapon from the ashes.

Savage blew out a low curse behind him. "Four Breed males gone Rogue in the same city on the same night? No one's seen those kind of numbers in the past twenty years."

Jehan nodded. He'd been a youth at that time, but more than old enough to remember firsthand. "Let's hope we never see bloodshed again like we did back then, Sav."

And all the more reason to take Opus Nostrum out at the root. For Jehan, a Breed male who'd spent a lot of his privileged life in pursuit of one pleasure or another, he couldn't think of any higher calling than his place among the Order.

He cleaned his dagger and sheathed it on the weapons belt of his black patrol fatigues. "Come on," he said to Savage. "I saw Trygg ash one of these four a few blocks back. Let's go find him and make sure we don't have any witnesses in need of a mind-scrub before we report back to Commander Archer at headquarters."

They pivoted to leave the alley together—only to find they were no longer alone there.

Another Breed male stood at the mouth of the narrow passage. Dark-eyed, with a trimmed black beard around the grim line of his mouth, the vampire was dressed in a black silk tunic over loose black pants tucked into gleaming black leather boots that rose nearly to his knees.

The only color he wore was a striped sash of vibrant, saffron-and-cerulean silk tied loosely around his waist. Family colors. Formal colors, reserved for the solemnest of old traditions.

Jehan couldn't bite back his low, uttered curse.

Beside him in the alleyway, Savage moved his fingers toward his array of weapons.

"It's all right." Jehan stayed his comrade's hand with a pointed shake of his head. "Naveen is my father's emissary."

In response, the dark-haired male inclined his head. "Greetings, Prince Jehan, noble eldest son of Rahim, the just and honorable king of the Mafakhir tribe."

The courtly bow that followed set Jehan's teeth and fangs on edge almost as much as his official address. From within the folds of his tunic, Naveen withdrew a sealed piece of parchment. The royal messenger held it out to Jehan in sober, expectant silence.

A stamped, red wax seal rode the back of the official missive...just like the one Jehan had received in this same manner a year ago.

A year and a day ago, he mentally amended.

For a moment, Jehan just stood there, unmoving.

But he knew Naveen had been sent with specific orders to deliver the sealed message, and it would dishonor the male deeply if he failed in that mission.

Jehan stepped forward and took the stiff, folded parchment from Naveen's outstretched hand. As soon as it was in Jehan's possession, the royal messenger pivoted and strode back into the darkness without another word.

In the silence that followed, Savage gaped. "What the fuck was that all about?"

"Family business. It's not important." Jehan slipped the document into the waistband of his pants without opening it.

"It sure as hell looked important to that guy." When Jehan started walking out of the alley, Sav matched his clipped pace. "What is it? Some kind of royal subpoena?"

Jehan grunted. "Something like that."

"Aren't you going to read it?"

Jehan shrugged. "There's no need. I know what it says."

Sav arched a blond brow. "Yeah, but I don't."

To satisfy his friend's curiosity, Jehan retrieved the sealed message and passed it over to him. "Go ahead."

Sav broke the seal and unfolded the parchment, reading as he and Jehan turned down another narrow street. "It says someone died. A mated couple, killed together in a plane crash a year ago."

Jehan nodded grimly, already well aware of the couple's tragic demise. News of their deaths had been the reason for the first official notice he'd received from his father.

Savage read on. "This says the couple—a Breed male from the Mafakhir tribe and a Breedmate from another tribe, the Sanhaja, had been blood-bonded as part of a peace pact between the families."

Jehan grunted in acknowledgment. The pact had been in place for centuries, the result of an unfortunate chain of events that had spawned a bloody conflict between his family and their closest neighbors, the Sanhajas. After enough blood had been spilled on both sides, a truce was finally declared. A truce that was cemented with blood spilled by another means.

An eternal bond, shared between a male from Jehan's line and a Breedmate from the rival tribe.

So long as the two families were bound together by blood, there had been peace. The pact had never been broken. The couple who perished in the plane crash had been the sole link between the families in the modern age. With their deaths, the pact was in limbo until a new couple came together to revive the bond.

Savage had apparently just gotten to the part of the message Jehan had been dreading for the past twelve months. "It says here that in accordance with the terms of that pact, if the blood bond is severed and no other couple elects to carry it forward within the term of a year and a day, then the eldest unmated son of the eldest Breed male of the Mafakhir tribe and the unmated Breedmate nearest the age of thirty from the Sanhaja tribe shall..."

Sav's long stride began to slow, then it stopped altogether. He swiveled his head in Jehan's direction. "Holy shit. Are you kidding me? You're being drafted to go home to Morocco and take a mate?"

A scowl furrowed deep into his brow at the very thought. "According to ritual, I am."

His comrade let out a bark of a laugh. "Well, shit. Congratulations, Your Highness. This is one lottery I'm happy as hell I won't be winning."

Jehan grumbled a curse in reply. Although he didn't find much humor in the situation, his friend seemed annoyingly amused.

Sav was still chuckling as they resumed their march up the alleyway. "When is this joyous occasion supposed to take place?"

"Tomorrow," Jehan muttered.

There was a period of handfasting with the female in question, but the details of the whole process were murky. In truth, he'd never paid much attention to the fine print of the pact because he hadn't imagined there would be a need to know.

He didn't really expect he needed to understand it now either, as he had no intention of participating in the antiquated exercise. But like it or not, he respected his father too much to disgrace him or the family by refusing to respond to their summons.

So it seemed he had little choice but to return to the family Darkhaven in Morocco and deliver his regrets in person.

He could only hope his father might respect his prodigal eldest son enough to free him from this ridiculous obligation and the unwanted shackle that awaited him at the end of it.

CHAPTER 2

Eighteen hours later and fresh off his flight to Casablanca, Jehan sat in the passenger seat of his younger brother's glossy black Lamborghini as it sped toward the Mafakhir family Darkhaven about an hour outside the city.

"Father didn't think you'd come." Marcel glanced at Jehan briefly, his forearm slung casually over the steering wheel as the sleek Aventador ate up the moonlit stretch of highway, prowling past other vehicles as if they were standing still. "I have to admit, I wasn't sure you'd actually show up either. Only Mother seemed confident you wouldn't just tear up the message and send it back home with Naveen as confetti."

"I didn't realize that was an option."

"Very funny," Marcel replied with another sidelong look.

Jehan turned his attention to the darkened desert landscape outside the window. He'd been questioning his sanity in answering the family summons even before he'd left Rome.

His Order team commander, Lazaro Archer, hadn't been enthused to hear about the obligation either, especially when things were heating up against Opus Nostrum and a hundred other pressing concerns. Jehan had assured Lazaro that the unplanned leave was merely a formality and that he'd be back on patrol as quickly as possible—without the burden of an unwanted Breedmate in tow.

Marcel maneuvered around a small convoy of humanitarian supply trucks, no doubt on their way to one of the many remote villages or refugee camps that had existed in this part of the world for centuries. Once the road opened up, he buried the gas pedal again.

If only they were heading away from the family compound at breakneck speed, rather than toward it.

"Mother's had the entire Darkhaven buzzing with plans and arrangements ever since you called last night." Marcel spoke over the deep snarl of the engine. "I can't remember the last time I've seen her so excited."

Jehan groaned. "I'm here, but that doesn't mean I intend to go through with any of this."

"What?" Jehan looked over and found his only sibling's face slack with incredulity. His light blue eyes, so like Jehan's own—a color inherited from their French beauty of a mother—were wide under Marcel's tousled crown of brown waves. "You have to go through with it. There's no blood bond between the Mafakhirs and the Sanhajas anymore. Not since our cousin and his Breedmate died a year ago."

When Jehan didn't immediately acknowledge the severity of the problem, his brother frowned. "If a year and a day should pass without a natural mating occurring between the families, the terms of the pact specifically state—"

"I know what they state. I also know those terms were written up during a very different time. We don't live in the Middle Ages anymore." *And thank fuck for that,* he mentally amended. "The pact is a relic that needs to be retired. Hopefully it won't take too much convincing to make our father understand that."

Marcel went quiet as they veered off the highway and set a course for the rambling stretch of desert acreage that comprised their family's Darkhaven property. In a few short minutes, they turned onto the private road.

The family lands were lush and expansive. Thick clusters of palm trees spiked black against the night sky, small oases amid the vast spread of dark, silken sand. Up ahead was the iron gate and tall brick perimeter wall that secured the massive compound where Jehan had grown up.

Even before they approached the luxurious Darkhaven, his feet twitched inside his boots with the urge to run.

While they paused outside the gate and waited to be admitted inside, Marcel pivoted in his seat toward Jehan. His youthful, twenty-four-year-old face was solemn. "The pact has never been broken. You know that, right? Not once in all of the six-and-a-half centuries it's been in place. It's not a relic. It's tradition. That kind of thing may not be sacred to you, but it is to our parents. It's sacred to the Sanhajas too."

His brother was so earnest, maybe there was another way to dodge this bullet. "If you feel that strongly about it, why don't you pick up the torch instead? Take my place and I can turn around right now and go back to my work with the Order."

"Ohh, no." He vigorously shook his head. "Even if I wanted to—which I don't—without another mated couple occurring naturally between our families, the pact calls for the eldest son of the eldest male of our line. That means you. Besides, there are worse fates. Seraphina Sanhaja is a gorgeous woman."

Seraphina. It was the first time he'd heard the name of his intended. A silken, exotic name. Just the sound of it made Jehan's blood course a bit hotter in his veins. He dismissed the sensation with a sharp sigh as he stared at his brother. He couldn't deny that a part of him was intrigued to know more. "You've seen her?"

Marcel nodded. "She and her sister, Leila, are both stunning."

Not surprising, considering they were Breedmates. Although they didn't have the vampiric traits of Jehan's kind, the half-human, half-Atlantean females called Breedmates were flawless beauties without exception. His Paris-born mother was testament to that. As was Lazaro Archer's flame-haired Breedmate back in Rome, Melena.

"So, what's wrong with her, then?" Jehan murmured. "Let me guess. She's a miserable, bickering shrew? Or is it worse, a meek little mouse who's afraid of her own shadow?"

"She's neither." Marcel grinned as he eased the Lamborghini through the opened gates. "She's lovely, Jehan. You'll see for yourself soon enough."

"Not if I have anything to say about that." Crossing his arms, he sat back in the buttery soft leather seat. "I have a return flight to Rome tomorrow. I figure that gives me plenty of time to convey my regrets to our parents and get the hell out of here."

"You can't do that. Everything is already in motion. I told you, arrangements were made right after you called."

Jehan cursed under his breath. "If I'd realized our parents would charge forward without asking me, I could've saved everyone the effort. I should've told them over the phone that I wasn't interested in any of this and stayed put in Rome. Unfortunately, it's too late for that now. Whatever arrangements have been made will need to be canceled."

"I don't think you understand, brother." Marcel slowed the car as they rolled onto the half-moon drive of the Darkhaven's impressive arched entrance. "The handfast begins tomorrow. Which means the families assemble for the official meet-and-greet tonight. There will be formal introductions, followed by the traditional garden walk at midnight, and the turning of the hourglass to mark the celebratory commencement and the start of the handfast period."

Jehan's unfamiliarity with the process must have been as apparent as his disinterest. Marcel frowned at him. "You don't have any idea what I'm talking about, do you? For fuck's sake, the pact's been in place for centuries, but you never took the time to study the terms?"

"I've been busy."

Marcel's lips quirked at the droll reply, but it was clear that he took the pact seriously. Apparently everyone did, aside from Jehan.

For an instant, he felt a pang of loss for his absence all these years. It had been his choice to leave, his choice to make his own way in the world instead of being satisfied with the privileged, if stifling, one he'd been handed at birth. He'd yearned more for adventure than tradition, and supposed he always would.

"So, this handfast entails what, exactly?"

"A period of eight nights, spent together in seclusion. No visitors, no communication with the outside world in any form. Just the two of you, alone at the oasis retreat on the border of our lands and the Sanhajas'."

"In other words, imprisonment for a week and a day with a female who may or may not be a willing party to this whole forced seduction ritual. Followed by what—a public blood bond encouraged at sword point?"

"Forced seduction? Public blood bond?" Marcel gaped at him as if he'd lost his mind. "The handfast is all about consent, Jehan. Touch Seraphina against her wishes and her family has the right to take your head. Drink her blood without her permission and no one would balk if the Sanhajas took out their revenge on the entire Mafakhir tribe. This is serious shit."

Not to mention, archaic. Even though he had no plans to touch Seraphina Sanhaja or any other female who wasn't of his own choosing, Jehan's curiosity was piqued. "I thought the whole point of the pact was to seal the peace between our two families with a blood bond."

"It is," Marcel said. "But only if the handfast is successful."

"Meaning?"

"There has to be a mutual agreement. There has to be love. If there's no desire to bond as a mated couple at the end of the handfast, the couple is free to go their separate ways and the pact then moves on to the next pair in line."

"So, there's an out clause?" Jehan's brows rose in surprise. "That's the best news I've heard all night."

His brother released a frustrated-sounding breath. "I don't know why I'm bothering to explain any of this to you. The terms will be spelled out in detail at the ceremony tomorrow night."

The ceremony Jehan had no intention of attending.

Marcel parked in front of the opulent estate and killed the engine. The Aventador's scissor doors lifted upward and the two Breed males climbed out.

As they began to ascend the wide, polished stone steps leading to the Darkhaven's entrance, Jehan asked, "Who's the next pair in line after Seraphina and me?"

"That would be the Breedmate next nearest the age of thirty in the Sanhaja family, and the unmated eldest son of the second-eldest Breed male in our line. You remember our cousin, Fariq."

Jehan mentally recoiled. "Fariq, who prided himself on his collection of dead insects and snakes as a boy?"

Marcel chuckled. "He's not nicknamed Renfield for nothing."

And Jehan couldn't help but feel guilty that his refusal of the pact would mean some unfortunate Breedmate would eventually have to spend eight nights alone with the repulsive male.

But he didn't feel guilty enough to let the farce continue. He had to halt the whole thing before it went any further.

"Father's waiting for you in his study," Marcel told him as they reached the top. "Everyone else is in the main salon, where the formal introductions will be made."

Alarm shot through him at that last announcement. Jehan grabbed his brother's muscled arm. "Everyone else?"

"Mother and the Sanhajas. And Seraphina, of course."

Ah, fuck. If he thought this was bad enough before he stepped off the plane tonight, the situation had just nose-dived into a disaster zone. "They're here right now? All of them?"

"That's what I've been telling you. Everything is already in motion and ready to begin. We were only waiting for you to arrive, brother."

CHAPTER 3

The sound of deep male voices carried from the foyer. Until that moment, the small gathering inside the Darkhaven's elegant salon had been engaged in pleasant chatter about the weather and a dozen other light subjects. But at the low rumble of muffled conversation somewhere outside the gilded walls, a palpable spike of anticipation pierced the atmosphere in the room.

"Ah, my sons have finally arrived." Beautiful and poised, Simone Mafakhir smiled from her seat on a silk divan, her sky blue eyes lit with excitement. "I know Jehan will be delighted to meet you, Seraphina."

Sera's mouth was suddenly too dry to speak, but she gave a polite nod and returned the brunette Breedmate's warm smile.

"Seraphina's talked of little else all day," her mother said, giving Sera's hand a pat from her seat beside her on a velvet sofa opposite Simone. "She's been full of curiosity about Jehan ever since she arrived back home this morning."

On the other side of Sera, her blonde, twenty-two-year-old sister, Leila, barely stifled a giggle.

It was true. Sera had been full of questions since she'd been called home by her parents. She still didn't know much about Jehan, other than the fact that he'd flown in tonight from Rome, where he'd been living for many years. And that he'd come because he had been summoned to fulfill his role in the ancient handfasting pact that had existed between their families for half a dozen centuries.

The same as she had.

That is, if she managed to make it through the evening without bolting for the nearest escape.

She pressed the back of her hand to her forehead, which had gone suddenly clammy. Her heart was racing, and her lungs felt as if they were suddenly caught in a vise.

She stood up, not quite steady on the high heels she wasn't accustomed to wearing. The flouncy, blush-pink dress she'd borrowed from Leila on her sister's insistence swayed around her knees as she wobbled, lightheaded and fighting the wave of nausea that rose up on her.

"Would it be possible to, um...freshen up for a moment?"

"Yes, of course," Simone replied. "There's a powder room just down the hall."

Her parents both looked at her in genuine concern. "Are you all right, darling?" her mother asked.

"Yes." Sera gave them a weak nod that only made her wooziness worse. "I'm fine, really."

She just needed to get the hell out of there before she passed out or threw up.

Leila stood and grabbed her elbow. "I'll go with you."

They hurried out of the room together, Sera practically leaving her sister in her wake. Once safely enclosed in the large powder room, Sera sagged against the back of the door.

"What on earth is wrong with you?" Leila whispered.

Sera swallowed back a building scream. "I can't do this. I thought maybe I could—for our parents, since it's obviously so important to them—but I can't. I mean, this whole situation...the pact, the handfasting? It's insane, right? I never should have agreed to any of this."

It was all happening too quickly. Yesterday morning, an e-mail from her parents had reached her at the remote outpost where she'd been working. The message had been short and cryptic, telling her that she was needed at home immediately.

Terrified with concern, she'd dropped everything and raced back—only to learn that the emergency requiring her presence was a musty old agreement that would send her away with a complete stranger. A Breed male who may not understand or care that her carotid wasn't up for grabs, regardless of what the pact between their families might imply.

Oh, God. Her stomach started to spin again. She pressed her hand to her abdomen and took a steadying breath.

She paced the cramped powder room, her voice beginning to rise. "I need to get out of here. I can't do this, Leila. I must've been out of my mind for even considering coming here tonight."

Her sister stared at her patiently, her soft green eyes sympathetic as she let Sera vent. "You're just nervous. I would be too. But I don't think you're crazy for being here. And I don't think the agreement between our families is insane, either." She swept a blonde tendril behind her ear and shrugged. "It's endured all these years for a reason. Actually, I think it's kind of romantic."

"Romantic?" Sera scoffed. "What's romantic about a truce struck after years of bloodshed resulting from the kidnap of a virgin Breedmate from our tribe by a barbarian Breed male from theirs six-hundred years ago?"

Leila let out a sigh. "Things were different back then. And it's romantic because they fell in love."

Sera arched her brows in challenge. "Tragic, because despite their blood bond, they both died in the end and set off a long, violent war."

Sera knew the whole, tragic story as well as her sister did. It was practically legend in the Sanhaja family. And if she was being honest, there was a part of her that ached for that long-dead couple and their doomed love.

But it didn't change the fact that centuries later, here she was, standing in a locked bathroom in a borrowed dress and high-heeled sandals, while just down the hall, a Breed male she'd never even met before was expecting her to go away with him for eight long nights—all in their parents' shared hopes that they might come back madly in love and bound by blood for eternity.

Ridiculous.

Sera shook her head. "It might've been true centuries ago that the best way to guarantee peace was to turn an enemy into family," she conceded. "But that was then and this is now. There hasn't been conflict between the Mafakhirs and our family for decades."

Leila tilted her head. "And how do you know that's not because the pact was in place all that time? Since it first began, there's never been a time when there wasn't at least one mated pair between our families. Until now. What if the pact really is the only thing keeping the peace? It's never been broken or tested, Sera. Do you really want to be the first one to try?"

For a moment, hearing her sister's emphatic reply, Seraphina almost bought into the whole myth. At twenty-seven, she was a practical, independent woman who knew her own mind as well as her own worth, but there was a small part of her—maybe a part of every woman—who still wanted to believe in fairy tales and romance stories.

She wanted to believe in eternal love and happy endings, but that's not what awaited her on the other side of the powder room door.

"The pact isn't magic. And the handfast isn't romantic. It's all a bunch of silly, outdated nonsense."

"Well, call it what you will," Leila murmured. "I think it's charming."

"I doubt you'd be so enthusiastic if you were the one being yanked out of your world and all the things that matter to you, only to be dropped into some strange male's lap as his captive plaything." Sera considered her dreamy-eyed younger sister. "Or maybe you would."

Leila laughed and shook her head. "The handfast is only for a week. And you won't be dropped into anyone's lap or held against your will. You're meant to get to know each other away from the distractions of the outside world. That's all. Handfasting at the oasis retreat is symbolic more than anything else. Besides, I can think of worse things than spending a week in beautiful surroundings, getting to know a handsome Breed male. One who also happens to be a prince."

Sera scoffed. "A prince in name only. The old tribes of this region aren't any more royal than you or me." Which they weren't. Adopted by Omar and Amina Sanhaja as infants from orphanages for the indigent, there was no chance of that. Sera cocked a curious look on her sister. "How do you know Jehan's handsome? I thought you've never met him."

"I haven't. But being Breed, he's sure to have his mother's chestnut brown hair and incredible blue eyes. The same as his brother, Marcel."

Sara rolled her eyes. "Well, I don't care what he looks like and I don't care about his pedigree either. I'm not looking for a mate, and if I was, I certainly wouldn't be going about it this way."

Yet despite all of that—despite her unwillingness to be part of some antiquated agreement that had long outlived its expiration date as far as she was concerned—she knew she couldn't walk away from her obligation to her family.

Honoring the pact was important to her parents, which made it important to her as well.

And there was another, more selfish reason she had finally conceded to come.

Several hundred thousand reasons. The amount of her trust fund, which her father had agreed to release to her early. She would have it all at the end of the week—after her handfast with Jehan Mafakhir was over.

Sera needed that money.

As much as her father loved her, he knew she wouldn't be able to turn away from what he had offered. Not when there was so much she could do with that kind of gift.

That didn't mean she had to like it.

Nor did it mean she had to like Jehan Mafakhir.

In fact, she was determined to avoid him as much as possible for the duration of their confinement together. If she was lucky, maybe they wouldn't even need to speak to each other.

Miserable with the whole idea, she exhaled a slow, defeated sigh. "It's only for eight nights, right?"

Leila nodded, then her eyes went wide at the sound of measured footsteps and deep voices in the hallway. Putting a finger to her lips, she cracked open the door and peered out. She reported to Sera in a hushed whisper. "Jehan just walked into the salon with his father and Marcel. You can't leave him waiting. We have to get out of here right now!"

The bubble of anxiety Sera had been fighting suddenly spiked into hot panic. "So soon? I thought I'd have a few more minutes before—"

"Now, Sera! Let's go!" Grabbing her by the arm, Leila opened the door and ushered her outside. As they moved toward the salon, Leila leaned in close to whisper next to Sera's ear. "And I was right, by the way. He's beyond handsome."

CHAPTER 4

Jehan wasn't sure what had presented the most convincing argument for his consenting to take part in the handfasting: his brother's earnest persuasion on the ride to the Darkhaven, or his father's stoic greeting and his resulting obvious, if unspoken, expectation that his eldest son would shirk his obligation to the family.

If he'd been met with furious demands that he must pick up the mantle of responsibility concerning the pact with the Sanhajas, it would have been the easiest thing for Jehan to pivot on his heels and hoof his way back to Casablanca to catch the earliest flight back to Rome.

But his father hadn't blown up or slammed his fists into his desk when Jehan arrived in his study a few minutes ago to explain that he wanted no part in the duty waiting for him in the salon. Rahim Mafakhir had listened in thoughtful silence. Then he'd simply stood up and walked toward the door of his study without a word.

Not that he'd needed to speak. His lack of reaction spoke volumes.

He'd been anticipating Jehan's refusal.

He'd been fully prepared for his prodigal son to let him and the rest of the family down.

And as much as Jehan had wanted to pretend he was okay with that, the fact was, it had stung.

It had been at that precise moment—his father's strong hand wrapped around the doorknob, his stern face grim with disappointment—that Jehan had blurted out words he was certain he'd live to regret.

"I'll do it," he'd said. "Eight nights with the Sanhaja female, as the pact requires. Nothing more. Then, after the handfast is over and my duty is fulfilled, I'll go back to Rome and the pact can move on to the next of our kin in line to heed the call."

Now, as Jehan entered the salon with his father and Marcel, he felt a small spark of hope.

She wasn't there. Only his mother and an anxious-looking couple he assumed was Omar and Amina Sanhaja. No sign of the unmated Breedmate he was supposed to formally meet tonight.

Holy shit. Dare he hope the Sanhajas' daughter had called a stop to this farce?

"Here we are!" An exuberant voice sounded brightly from behind him, killing his hope before it had a chance to fully catch fire.

The voice belonged to a leggy blonde with a megawatt smile and pretty, pale green eyes. Attractive. Certainly cheerful and energetic. As far as temporary housemates went, Marcel was right—there were worse sentences he could endure.

The blonde paused to glance behind her, and that was when Jehan realized his error.

"Come on, Seraphina!" She grabbed the hand of a tall, curvy brunette who'd hesitated momentarily just outside the threshold. "Don't be shy. Everyone's waiting for you."

The blonde was lovely, as Marcel had assured him. But her reserved, darker-haired sister was something far more than that.

Blessed with the figure of a goddess and the face of an angel, when she appeared in the doorway, Jehan could barely keep from gaping. He glanced briefly to his brother and met Marcel's *I-told-you-so* grin.

Damn.

Seraphina Sanhaja was, in a word, extraordinary.

Framed by a mane of cascading brown curls, a pair of long-lashed eyes the color of rich sandalwood flecked with gold lifted to meet Jehan's arrested gaze. Her face was heart-shaped and delicate, an exotic artistry of fine bones and smooth, sun-kissed olive skin that glowed with rising pink color as she stared at him.

How this stunning woman had managed to get past the age of twenty without some other Breed male locking her into a blood bond, Jehan couldn't even imagine.

His pulse stirred at the sight of her, sending heat into his veins. Even though he wasn't in the market for a mate, as a hot-blooded Breed male, it was impossible to deny his body's intense reaction to the female. He drew in a slow breath, his acute senses taking in the cinnamon-sweet scent of her and the subtle uptick of her heartbeat as he held her in his unblinking gaze.

For a moment, he was sorry he didn't have any use for tribal laws or ancient pacts that would put Seraphina Sanhaja in his company—better yet, in his bed—for the next eight nights.

Her sister tugged her forward on a light giggle. "Isn't this exciting?"

Where Leila crackled with unbridled enthusiasm, Seraphina was nearly impossible to read. Her lush lips pursed a bit as she made a silent study of him, her expression carefully schooled, inscrutable.

Standing before him, she was reticent and aloof.

Assessing and...*unimpressed?*

Jehan's brows lifted. He didn't want to admit the jab his ego took at her apparent lack of interest in him. With his thick, shoulder-length dark hair, tawny skin and light blue eyes, he'd never been at a loss for female attention.

Oh, hell. What did he care if she didn't like what she saw? The week ahead was going to pass a hell of a lot faster if he didn't have to spend it with a blushing, eyelash-batting Breedmate who couldn't wait to surrender her carotid to him.

Jehan stared her down ruthlessly as the formal introductions were made.

He was still trying to figure her out after what seemed like endless polite, if awkward conversation in the salon. Their parents made pleasant small talk together. Marcel and Leila fell into easy chatter about books and music and current events, both of them clearly striving to bring Jehan and Seraphina into the discussion.

It wasn't working.

Jehan's thoughts were back with his team in Rome. When he'd spoken earlier tonight with Lazaro Archer, he'd learned that rumors were circulating about Opus Nostrum moving weapons across Europe and possibly into Africa.

Even though he was only going to be delayed from his missions with the Order for a week, he already itched to be suited up in his patrol gear and weapons, not stuffed into the white button-down, dark trousers, and gleaming black dress shoes he'd worn from the airport.

As for Seraphina, Jehan got the feeling she was only seconds away from making a break for the nearest exit.

The otherwise cool and collected female jumped when the clock struck twelve. Smiled wanly as her mother erupted into excited applause.

"It's time!" Amina Sanhaja crowed from across the room. "Go on now, you two. Go on!"

As their families began to urge them out of the salon together, Jehan slanted a questioning look on Seraphina.

"The midnight garden stroll," she murmured under her breath, the first thing she'd said to him directly all night. She stared at him as if annoyed that she needed to explain. "It's part of the tradition."

Ah, right. Marcel had mentioned something about that in the car when Jehan was only half-listening. He'd much rather watch Seraphina's mouth explaining it to him again.

She softly cleared her throat. "At midnight, we're supposed to walk together privately to mark the turning of the hourglass and the beginning of our—"

"Sentence?" he prompted wryly.

Surprise arched her fine brows.

Jehan smirked and gestured for her to walk ahead of him. "Please, after you."

With their parents and siblings crowding the salon doorway behind them, he and Seraphina left the room and headed down the hallway, toward a pair of arched glass doors leading out to the moonlit gardens behind the Darkhaven estate.

The night was cool and crisp in the desert, and infinitely dark. Above them stars glittered and a half-moon glowed milky white against an endless black velvet sky.

It might have been romantic, if the woman walking alongside him didn't take each delicate step as if she was being led to the gallows. She glanced behind them for about the sixth time in as many minutes.

"Are they still there?" Jehan asked.

"Yes," she said. "All of them are standing in front of the glass, watching us."

He could fix that. "Come with me."

Taking her elbow in a loose hold, he ducked off the main garden path with her to one of the many winding paths that crisscrossed the manicured topiary and flowering, fragrant hedges.

The sweet perfume of jasmine and roses laced the night air, but it was another scent—cinnamon and something far more exotic—that made him inhale a bit deeper as he brought Seraphina to a more private section of the gardens.

She hung back a few paces, following him almost hitchingly in her strappy high heels. When he glanced over his shoulder, he found her pretty face pinched in a frown. Then she stopped completely and shook her head. "This is far enough."

"Relax, Seraphina. I'm not going to push you into the hibiscus and ravish you."

Her eyes widened for a second, but then her frown narrowed into an affronted scowl. "That's not why I stopped. These shoes...they're killing my feet."

Jehan walked back to her. Eyeing the tall spikes, he exhaled a low curse. "I don't doubt they're killing you. In the right hands, those things could be deadly weapons."

She smiled—a genuine, heart-stopping smile that was there and gone in an instant.

"Hold on to my shoulder."

Her fingers came to rest on him, generating a swift, unexpected electricity in his veins. Jehan tried to ignore the feel of her touch as he reached down and lifted her left foot into his hands. He unfastened the pretty, but impractical, shoe and slipped it off.

Her satisfied sigh as he freed her bare foot went through him even more powerfully than her touch. Gritting his teeth to discourage his fangs from punching out of his gums in heated response, Jehan made quick work of her other shoe, then stepped away from her.

"Better?" His voice had thickened. Along with another part of his anatomy.

"Much better." She was looking at him cautiously as she took the pair of sandals from where they dangled off his fingertips. "Thank you."

"My pleasure." And it was. More than he might have wanted to admit. He cocked his head at her. "How old are you, Seraphina?"

"Excuse me?"

He immediately felt rude for asking, but there was a part of him that wanted to know. Needed to know. "We're supposed to be getting to know each other, aren't we?"

The reminder seemed to calm some of her indignation. "I'm twenty-seven. Why do you want to know?"

"I just wonder why you aren't already mated and blood-bonded. You were raised in a Darkhaven, so you must know many Breed males. If any of the ones I know ever saw you, there'd be at least a hundred of them beating a path to your door."

She stared at him for a moment in uncertain silence, then shrugged. "Maybe I prefer human men."

Shit. He hadn't even considered that. "Do you?"

"To be honest, I haven't given the idea of a blood bond a lot of thought. My life is full and I keep busy enough with other things."

She started walking away from him, her bare feet moving softly, fluidly, along the bricked path. And he couldn't help noticing she hadn't really answered his question.

He strode up next to her. "What kind of things have kept you so busy that you're still unmated and nearing the ripe old age of thirty?"

She scoffed, but there was humor in her tone. "Important things."

"Such as?"

"I volunteer at some of the border camps, taking care of people who've been displaced by wars and other disasters. I guess you could say it's been something of a calling for me."

Well, he hadn't been expecting that. Granted, she didn't seem the type to flutter around in fancy dresses and high-heeled sandals all day, but he also wouldn't have imagined a stunning woman like her spending her time covered in dust and sweat. Or putting herself in harm's way in those turbulent areas that had never known peace, even before the wars between the humans and the Breed.

"What about you, Jehan?"

"What about me?"

"For starters, how old are you?"

"Thirty-three."

She glanced at him. "Younger than I expected. But then it's impossible to guess a Breed male's age. It's always seemed unfair to me that your kind never looks older than thirty, even the Gen Ones who've been around for centuries."

Jehan lifted his shoulder. "A small consolation for the fact that we can never put our faces in the sunlight. Unlike your kind."

"Hm. I guess that's true." She tilted her head at him. "What exactly do you do in Rome?"

"I'm part of the Order. Captain of my unit," he added, not sure why he felt the need to impress her with his elevated rank.

She stopped dead in her tracks again, and something told him it didn't have anything to do with sore feet. A chill rolled off her as Jehan pivoted to look at her. She barked out a brittle laugh and shook her head. "No wonder they didn't tell me anything about you."

"Who?"

"My parents." Her arms crossed rigidly over her chest. "If they'd mentioned you were part of that brutal organization, there's no way in hell I would've agreed to any of this. No matter what leverage they used to try to convince me."

Jehan's suspicions rankled along with his pride. "You have a problem with the Order?"

"I have a problem with cold-blooded killers."

Was she serious? "My brethren and I are not—"

She didn't let him finish. "I've devoted myself—everything I am— to saving lives. You're in the business of taking them." When he exhaled a tight curse and shook his head, she gave him a sharp look. "How many people have you killed?"

"Me personally, or—"

"I think that answers my question." She moved past him and started walking away at a swift clip.

He caught up in a handful of strides. "There's nothing cold-blooded about what the Order does. Are we brutal sometimes? Only when there's no other choice. But we call it justice. We're protectors, not killers."

"Semantics."

"No, it's reality, Seraphina." When she didn't slow her pace, he reached out and caught her arm. She flinched at the contact. He wondered if it was purely out of indignation or the fact that even though a chill had expanded between them, the heat of attraction still sparked to life the instant they touched. Her pulse fluttered at the base of her elegant throat, her heart pounding so hard and fast he could feel it through his fingertips.

His entire body responded to that frantic drumming, his veins heating, his fangs prickling as they elongated behind his closed lips. His cock responded just as hungrily, pressing in demand against the zipper of his trousers.

She pulled out of his grasp. "I can't do this. You need to know that I have no interest in any kind of handfast, and I'm not looking for a blood bond. Especially with you."

Jehan drew back. "You don't want to be part of this because you just found out I belong to the Order?"

Her lush lips compressed into a flat line. "I never wanted to be part of it."

"That makes two of us."

"What?" She gaped at him.

He shook his head. "I only agreed out of obligation. Because I feel I owe it to my family to uphold their traditions, even if they don't mesh with mine."

Her breath rushed out of her. "Oh, thank God!"

She didn't hold back her relief. She sounded like a death row inmate suddenly granted a full pardon, and his pride took another ding to hear the depth of her alleviation. "So, what do we do now, Seraphina? Go back inside and tell them we're calling the whole thing off?"

"You mean, break the pact? We can't do that." She glanced down at the bricks at her feet. "I can't do that."

"Maybe it's time someone did."

He studied her under the thin light of the moon and stars overhead. Everything Breed in him was urging him to touch her—to lift her chin and sweep the loose tendrils of her curly brown hair away from her eyes, if only so he could see their unusual shade again. But he kept his hands to himself, fisting them at his sides when the desire to reach out nearly overrode his good sense.

"You strike me as a forward-thinking, intelligent woman. You don't actually believe the pact holds any kind of sway over the peace between our families anymore, do you?"

"No, I don't. But it's important to my parents, and that makes it important to me. But..." Finally, she lifted her head to meet his gaze. "There's another reason I agreed to the handfasting. I have a trust fund. A sizable one. It's not due to release to me until my thirtieth birthday, but my father's promised it to me early. At the end of the handfast."

"Ah." Jehan lifted his chin. He hadn't taken her for the type to be motivated by money, but he supposed there were worse things. "So, you're here on bribery, and I'm here out of some pointless obligation to prove to my father that I'm not his greatest disappointment."

"That's why you're here?"

Her voice was quiet, almost sympathetic. The soft look in her eyes threatened to unravel his thin control.

He gave a dismissive wave of his hand. "It doesn't matter why either of us are here. Apparently, we both just need to get through the next eight nights so we can get on with our real lives."

She nodded. "How are we going to do that?"

Looking at her standing so close to him in the cool night air, her beautiful face and tempting curves making his mouth water and his blood streak hot through his veins, Jehan wasn't sure how the hell he was going to survive a week of seclusion with her. Not without putting his hands or fangs—or any other part of his anatomy—within arm's reach of her.

One thing was certain. They would have to set some clear boundaries. Rigid boundaries that couldn't be crossed.

And rules.

Jehan let his gaze travel the length of her, desire hammering through every cell in his body.

Oh, yeah. To survive the next week alone with this female, he was going to need *a lot* of boundaries and rules.

CHAPTER 5

She should have said no.

She should have trusted her good sense and left Jehan standing in the middle of the midnight garden alone last night, not helped him set down terms of their own for the ritual neither of them wanted to be part of.

Instead, that next evening, she found herself seated beside him at the head of a long banquet room in her parents' Darkhaven in front of a combined hundred members of their two families who had assembled to celebrate their send-off and the start of the handfast's first night.

In less than an hour, she and Jehan would be delivered to the private oasis retreat and left to fend for themselves until officials from both tribes came to retrieve them at the end of the eight nights. Until then, she would be trapped with him in close quarters. Intimate quarters.

Oh, God. She must be out of her damn mind.

Sera reached for her wine glass and drained it in one gulp.

"Pace yourself," Jehan drawled from beside her. "If you get too tipsy, I'd hate to have to carry you out of here tonight."

"Like hell you will." She smiled and spoke under her breath, doing her best to pretend he wasn't the last male she'd ever choose to spend time with. "And we have a deal, remember? One that specifically states no touching. I expect you to honor that."

A chuckle emanated from him, so deep it was almost a growl. "Don't worry, I have no intention of touching you."

She placed her empty glass back on the table. "Good. Then don't even joke about it."

"Trust me, Seraphina, you'll know when I'm joking."

She made the mistake of looking at him and found him smirking as he leaned back in his chair. But there wasn't any humor in his light blue eyes. Only a dark promise that made her pulse skitter through her veins.

According to tradition, he was dressed in a white linen tunic and loose pants. A long, striped sash bearing his blue-and-gold family colors was tied around his trim waist. He looked decadent and confident, sprawled against the back of his seat. As arrogant as a prince accustomed to having the world bend to his whim, even if his title was as musty as the pact that bound her to him tonight.

As for Sera, she had been clothed according to tradition too. Wrapped and knotted into yards of diaphanous red silk that somehow formed a body-skimming gown, she was also dripping in beads and bangles. Painted henna patterns swirled in delicate flourishes and arcs over the backs of her hands and up her limbs.

The dress constricted her breathing and the decorations on her skin made her feel like an offering headed for the altar.

Jehan's searing gaze beside her wasn't helping.

Even though they'd agreed to avoid each other as much as possible for the next week, Sera couldn't forget the heat that had ignited between them in the garden. Or in the moment they'd first made eye contact in the Darkhaven's salon.

He was attractive; she couldn't begin to deny that. With his luxurious chestnut hair and impossibly blue eyes, he was heart-stoppingly gorgeous. The fact that his massive, muscular body and powerful presence seemed to suck all the air out of the room only made the handsome Breed male even more magnetic.

The V-neck of his linen tunic was cut several inches down his powerful chest, baring a lot of tawny skin and smooth muscle, and the edges of his Breed *dermaglyphs*. The color-infused skin markings indicated the vampire's mood, and right now, the neutral hues of Jehan's *glyphs* told her that he'd recently fed.

Not surprising. It was customary for a Breed male about to enter the handfast to slake his blood thirst on a willing human Host before the week began. This to ensure that he didn't drink from his Breedmate companion and bond to her out of physical need instead of love.

A vision of Jehan drinking from the throat of another woman sprang into Sera's mind uninvited. His dark head nestled into the curve of a tender neck. His sensual mouth fastened to smooth, pale skin as his sharp fangs penetrated a pounding vein and he began to drink his fill.

Would he gentle a woman with coaxing words and soothing

caresses when he took her carotid between his teeth? Or would he spring on her like the predator he was, dominating her with speed and force and white-hot power?

Some troubling part of her she didn't recognize stirred with the need to know.

Sera groaned. She squirmed in her seat as her pulse thudded faster and erotic warmth bloomed between her thighs.

She wanted to cross her legs to relieve the unwelcome ache, but the skirts of her ceremonial dress were too restricting. Elsewhere in the banquet room, her father was reciting the traditional terms of the handfast. She only half-listened, too distracted by Jehan's presence beside her and the heat of his gaze on her as she fidgeted and shifted in her chair.

It suddenly occurred to her that the room had gone strangely quiet. Expectantly quiet.

All eyes in the room were fixed on her, and her father was no longer speaking.

Jehan stood up and pointedly cleared his throat. "It's time for us to go, Seraphina."

"Oh." She rose to her feet, eager to escape the weight of everyone's gazes. Plus, she couldn't wait to put some much-needed distance between herself and Jehan.

But he wasn't moving. Why wasn't he moving?

"Don't forget the kiss!" someone shouted cheerfully from among the gathering. "It's tradition to seal the pact with a kiss!"

Leila. *Damn that girl.*

Sera shot a narrowed glare at her exuberant sibling but her grin showed no remorse.

"Kiss her!" she shouted again.

And then across the room, Marcel called for the kiss too. Someone else picked up the chant, then another. Before long, the entire place was applauding and thundering with the command. "Kiss her! Kiss her! Kiss her!"

Sera turned a miserable look on Jehan. "We don't really have t—"

Before she could finish, he moved closer and his mouth slanted over hers in a blast of heat. His lips caressed hers, impossibly soft, achingly sensual. His hands held her face, and yes, they were gentle. His kiss was too, but beneath its tenderness was a possessiveness—a raw power—that rocked her.

He mastered her mouth in an instant, and every brush of his lips had her aching to be claimed by him.

Her thoughts scattered. Her knees went a little boneless.

Even worse, the coil of warmth that had gathered between her thighs a few moments ago blazed molten and wild now.

Sera raised her hands to grip his shoulders, if only to keep from sagging against him in front of a hundred onlookers. All the reassurances of their private agreement to spend the next week in separate corners flew away like leaves on the wind as Jehan kissed her. She couldn't help it. She moaned against his mouth, her pulse quickening, hammering even louder than the cheers of the gathering around them.

Jehan released her abruptly. His blue eyes glittered with sparks of amber heat, their transformation making his desire all too clear. He ran his tongue over his wet lips and she saw the points of his fangs, now gleaming in his mouth like razor-sharp diamonds. His breath rasped out of him, rough and raw.

"Let's go," he growled for her ears only. "The sooner we get this damned farce over with, the better."

Then he took her by the hand and stalked away from the table with her in tow.

CHAPTER 6

Jehan's body was still rock hard and vibrating with lust more than an hour after he and Seraphina were delivered to the oasis retreat.

Holy hell. That kiss...

As short-lived and chaste as it had been, it had gripped him in a way that staggered him.

He hadn't been able to deny how attracted he was to Seraphina from the instant he laid eyes on her. Now he knew she wanted him too. Her response to their kiss had left no question about that. The color that had rushed up her throat and into her cheeks couldn't be blamed on anything else, nor could her soft little moans. He'd felt her desire for him. He'd breathed in the sweet scent of her arousal, felt it drumming in her blood.

His own blood had answered, and now that his mouth had sampled a taste of Seraphina's kiss, everything primal and male in him—everything Breed—pounded with a dark, dangerous need for more.

Somehow, he'd managed to rein it in back at the Darkhaven celebration.

Now, he just had to make sure to keep his desire in check for the duration of their confinement at the private villa.

Eight nights, that's all, he reassured himself.

One hundred and ninety-two hours, give or take the few that had already passed tonight.

Which meant somewhere around eleven thousand minutes. All of them to be spent in too-close quarters with a woman who lit up every nerve ending in his body like a flame set to dry tinder.

Yeah, the math wasn't helping.

Everything they might need had been provided for by their families.

Clothing, toiletries, a fully stocked kitchen for Seraphina. They would want for nothing from the outside world, and no one would interrupt their time together until the handfasting had ended.

They'd divvied up the place as soon as they'd been dropped off, negotiating territory and establishing boundaries where neither of them would cross. It only seemed right to give her the privacy of the massive bedroom. As for Jehan, he would inhabit the general living quarters, and use the big nest of cushions in the main room as his bed for the next week.

With Seraphina settling into the sole bedroom suite on her own, Jehan prowled the open space of the villa like a caged cat, taking stock of the unfamiliar surroundings. He strode across richly dyed rugs spread over terra cotta tiled floors. Above his head, the high, domed ceiling glowed with soft golden lights that glinted off a mosaic of gem-colored glass embedded into the white stucco plaster.

Down the wing of the hallway opposite the bedroom where Seraphina had sequestered herself was a traditional bathing room with a steaming, spring-fed pool surrounded by silk-draped columns and fat pillar candles.

In the adjacent, open-concept chamber, more beds of cushions and pillows were arranged around the room, some steeped in shadows, others strategically placed in front of tall, ornately framed mirrors. Erotic statuary and tables holding bottles of perfumed oils and incense jars completed the pleasure den.

Jehan frowned, shaking his head. The handfast agreement may forbid a male from forcing himself on the Breedmate sent with him to this place, but every room in the villa was obviously designed with sex and seduction in mind.

And try as he might to resist imagining Seraphina reclined on those cushions or stepping naked out of the steam-clouded baths, his mind refused to obey.

Eight nights.

He would be lucky to make it through this first one without losing his mind or tearing down the bedroom door she was currently hiding behind on the other side of the villa.

He needed fresh air. What he really needed was a hundred-foot wall between him and his unwanted roommate. A length of sturdy chain wouldn't hurt either.

Jehan walked back out to the main living area and headed for the

French doors leading out to an oasis patio in back. As he crossed the room, he heard Seraphina hiss a curse from inside the bedroom.

He paused, listened. Told himself to keep walking in the opposite direction.

She swore again and he detoured for the passage leading to the bedroom.

"Are you all right in there?"

"Yes. Everything's fine." Her reply was quick, dismissively so.

He stood outside the closed door and heard her grumble in frustration. "I'm coming in."

"No. Wait—"

She stood in the center of the big room, tangled in the complicated yards of red silk that comprised her dress from the celebration. When he chuckled, she glowered. "It's not funny, you arrogant ass."

"Really?" He didn't even try to curb his grin. "Looks pretty funny from where I'm standing."

She huffed, narrowing a glare on him. "If you're going to stand there laughing at me, you might as well help."

He held up his hands. "No touching, remember? How can I help without breaking that part of our deal?" Of course, they'd also said no kissing, but that rule was already shot all to hell, even before they'd arrived tonight. "Ask me nicely and maybe I'll consider bending the rules."

Her shoulders sagged in defeat, but the baring of her straight, white teeth hardly looked submissive. "Jehan, will you please help me?"

He didn't want to admit how enticing his name sounded on her pretty lips. Especially when it involved asking him to assist in undressing her. His blood agreed, licking through his veins in eager anticipation as he stalked across the bedroom to where she stood.

She raised her right hand and gathered her long cascade of bead-strewn, soft brown curls off her neck as she presented her back to him. "There must be a dozen tiny knots holding this dress together. And I can't figure out where the ends of the long wrappings begin either."

Jehan stood behind her for a long moment, just looking. Just drinking in the sight of her graceful nape and elegant spine. She was blessed with hourglass curves and long, lean legs. The ceremonial dress hugged every inch of her in all the right places. Including the rounded swells of her beautiful ass.

How was it that his mouth could water, yet feel desert dry at the same time?

His gums prickled as his fangs swelled against his tongue. Another part of him was swelling too, pressing in carnal demand against the loose white linen of his pants. Heat rose in his blood and in his vision, swamping his irises with amber fire.

He reached out and began to loosen the first of the intricate knots.

There were eight of them, not a dozen. Each one was a test of his dexterity as well as his self-control. One by one, the fastenings fell away, baring Seraphina's naked back to his fevered gaze, inch by torturous inch.

Somewhere along the way, his lungs had stopped working. Desire raked him, sharp talons stealing his breath as he freed the last of the tiny knots and the scarlet silk slackened in his fingers.

Seraphina didn't seem to be breathing either. She stood unmoving, her mane of long hair still held aloft in her hand. Warmth poured off her skin, and he knew she had to feel his heat reaching out to her too.

Her heartbeat ticked frantically in the side of her neck, drawing his blazing eyes. The urge to stroke that tender pulse point—to touch and taste every enticing inch of her—nearly overwhelmed him.

Clamping his molars together, he fought to keep a grip on those urges. When he finally found his voice, it came out in a gravelly rasp. "There you go. All finished."

Seraphina paused, letting her hair fall. She turned a glance over her shoulder at him. "The wrappings too?"

Shit. He scowled and began a quick search for one of the ends of the lengths of silk. He tugged it loose and began to unwind it from around her bodice and waist. The damn thing was too long to pull free.

He swore and shook his head. "You'll have to turn with it."

"Like this?" She obeyed, pivoting in front of him. He nodded, then pulled the silk taut, letting the tail of it collect on the floor as she slowly spun before him. Around and around and around, her springy brown curls dancing as she turned, the beads threaded through the strands twinkling under the soft lights of the bedroom.

He couldn't take his eyes off her.

In some primitive part of his brain, he was the conquering desert warlord and she was his mesmerizing captive. His irresistible, stolen prize. He watched her spin, watched the ribbon of scarlet silk unwind, revealing more and more of the beautiful woman wrapped inside.

He wanted to keep undressing her.

When he looked at Seraphina, when he breathed in her cinnamon-sweet scent and felt the warmth of her skin with each dizzying turn she took in front of him... Damn him, but being near her like this, there was *so much* he wanted.

The drumming beat of her pulse vibrated in the small space between their bodies, and it made his own blood throb in answer. It made him hunger in a way he'd never fully known.

It made him want to burn the pact between their families and take her right here and now, willing or not.

Claim her.

Possess her in every way.

Make her his.

Dangerous thinking.

And a temptation he wasn't at all certain he would be able to resist.

Not for this one night, let alone seven more.

CHAPTER 7

She didn't know the exact moment when the air between them changed from simply hot and playful to something darker. Something so fierce and powerful, it made all of her nerve endings stand at full attention.

Jehan wanted her.

She'd have to be an idiot not to realize that.

She wanted him too.

And she was too smart to think for one second that he hadn't picked up on her staggering awareness of him as a man. As a dangerously seductive Breed male who could have her carotid caught in his teeth just as swiftly as he could have her legs parted beneath the driving pound of his muscular body.

Sera swallowed hard, her breath and heart racing as she slowed to a stop before him.

She glanced down, to where she was tethered to his strong hands by the unraveled length of red silk.

Although she was covered where it counted, there wasn't much of her dress left. Most of it lay on the floor at her feet; yards of scarlet pooled in the scant space between her body and Jehan's.

She licked her lips as she struggled for words. She should tell him to go, but everything female in her yearned for him to stay. She was no trembling virgin, no stranger to sex. But never with a Breed male. And the electricity that crackled to life between Jehan and her was something she'd never felt before.

It was arresting.

Consuming.

Terrifying in its intensity.

Yet it wasn't fear of him she felt when she held his piercing light blue eyes. It was fear of herself and of the way he made her feel. Fear of the things he made her want.

"Jehan, I..." She shook her head, unsure what she meant to say to him.

Leave?

Stay?

Forget the fact that neither one of them had come to this place willingly, nor intended to walk away from the archaic tradition with a blood-bonded mate?

But that's not what this moment was about.

What she saw in Jehan's amber-swamped gaze right now didn't have anything to do with their romantic surroundings or the expectation and hopes of their families. The things she was feeling had nothing to do with any of that either.

It was desire, pure and simple.

Immediate and intense.

Her body throbbed with it, longing pounding furiously in her breast and stirring a molten heat in the center of her. She drew a shallow breath—then held it tight as Jehan reached out to caress her cheek. His warm fingers felt hard and strong against her face, but he stroked her with such tenderness, she couldn't hold back the soft moan that spilled past her lips.

She stood rooted in place while her thoughts and emotions spiraled with rising anticipation.

The cool air of the room made her exposed skin feel even tighter. Her nipples ached behind the gauzy ribbons of silk that barely covered them. Goose bumps rose on her naked shoulders and arms with each second she endured under Jehan's hot, unwavering stare.

His fingers drifted away from her face slowly, then skated in a scorching trail down the side of her neck and onto the line of her left shoulder. She felt him trace the small red birthmark that rode her bicep—her Breedmate mark. His fingertips caressed the teardrop-and-crescent-moon symbol that signified she was something other than simply human.

That mark also meant that if she drank his blood, she would be bound to him and only him, for as long as either of them lived.

As if in answer to his touch, her veins vibrated with a primal quickening, pulse points throbbing in response to each tender stroke.

"You are...so incredibly beautiful." His deep voice was a growl of sound, tangling through his teeth and fangs. "But we made a deal, Seraphina."

She knew they had a deal. No looking. No touching. No physical contact of any kind. They had set clear boundaries and established separate corners where they could cohabitate for the week without having to spend any awkward time together. When the handfast was over, they would simply say their good-byes and return to their normal lives.

So why was she wishing so desperately that Jehan would pull her into his arms?

Why was she longing to feel the press of his muscled, hard body against her?

Why was the coil of smoldering need within her winding tighter, all of her nerve endings on fire and eager for more of his touch?

Eager for his kiss and everything that was certain to follow...

But he didn't kiss her.

A snarl curled up from the back of his throat. An animal sound. An otherworldly sound.

One of denial.

He shook his head, sending the thick waves of his dark hair swaying where they brushed his broad shoulders. His hand dropped away, down to his side. On a slow exhale, he stepped back, creating a cold vacuum of space between them.

He stooped to pick up the pool of red silk from the floor. He was retreating, yet when his gaze lifted to hers, his eyes still blazed with fiery desire, so hot it seared her. His fangs still glittered razor-sharp and hungered behind his lips.

He wanted her. It was written in his fierce expression and in the arousal that made itself obvious when she glanced down at the sizable bulge tenting his loose linen pants.

And he knew that she wanted him just as badly.

She could see that knowledge gleaming in his arrogant, knowing stare.

Damn him. He knew very well, and he was enjoying her torment!

He placed the mound of silk into her hands, a grin tugging at the corner of his mouth. "Goodnight, Seraphina."

He pivoted back toward the door. Then he strode out of the room without so much as a backward glance, leaving her to stare after him, half-dressed, fuming, and determined to avoid the infuriating ass for the duration of her confinement with him.

CHAPTER 8

For the next two days, he hardly saw Seraphina.

She spent her evenings behind the closed door of the massive bedroom suite, pointedly ignoring his existence. During the daytime, she slipped outside to the villa's sunbaked patio for hours on end, safely out of his reach and about as far away from his company as she could get.

She was pissed off, punishing him with frosty silence and deliberate avoidance.

Exactly as he'd intended when he'd left her high and dry—and as sexually frustrated as he was—that first night.

Better to earn her contempt than test his control under the desire-drenched heat of her gaze again. Her absence was a reprieve he welcomed. Better that than trying to withstand the temptation of her enticing curves and infinitely soft skin, now that he knew the pleasure of both.

Fuck. He'd only touched her for a few moments and the feel of her was branded into his fingertips. Her warmth and cinnamon-sugar scent was seared into his senses.

Even though she was out of sight now—rummaging quietly in the kitchen, by the sound of it—all he had to do was close his eyes and there she was in his mind. Standing in front of him in nothing but a few scraps of scarlet silk, her parted lips and heavy-lidded eyes inviting him to touch her. To take her.

No, pleading for him to do so.

But he'd shown her, right?

Pretending he was the one in control, denying both of them the pleasure they both wanted because he'd been too swamped with need to trust he could control himself. Now she was going to great lengths to ignore him, no doubt cursing him as a cold bastard. Meanwhile, he was walking around the villa like a caged animal with a semipermanent case of blue balls.

Damn.

He wasn't only a bastard. He was an idiot.

On a curse, he raked a hand through his hair and got up from the large floor cushion where he'd been unsuccessfully attempting to doze. It was just about sundown and he was twitchy with the need to be moving, to be doing something useful. Hell, he'd settle for doing anything at all.

He'd never been good at inactivity and the boredom of his exile was driving him insane.

More than once, he'd thought about slipping out in the middle of the night to run off some of his tension. Or say fuck the handfast and hoof it all the way to Casablanca and take the earliest flight to Rome.

With his Breed genetics, he could make it to the city in about as many hours as it would take to drive it. Maybe sooner.

Tempting.

But he couldn't leave Seraphina by herself out here. And as much as he wanted to get back to work going after Opus with his teammates at the Order, he wasn't about to abandon his honor or his family's by violating the terms of the pact.

If she could endure the week together and adhere to the ridiculous restrictions imposed on them by the ancient agreement—in addition to their own set of rules—then so could he.

And he supposed he really owed her an apology for the way he acted the other night.

Padding silently on his bare feet, Jehan strode toward the kitchen where he'd heard her a minute ago. She had her back to him, seated on an overstuffed sofa in the adjacent dining nook.

With her knees drawn up and her head bent down to study whatever she held in her hands, she didn't even notice him stealing up behind her from the kitchen. At first, he thought she'd taken one of the many books from the villa's library. But then he realized the small object was something else.

A phone.

In direct violation of the "no communication with the outside world" terms of the handfast.

The sneaky little rebel.

He opened his mouth to call her out on the breach, but then his acute sight caught the last few lines of a text message thread filling the display. Some guy named Karsten was asking her where she was and why she'd left him without saying where she'd gone. He was worried, he said. He needed her. Said he wasn't any good without her.

For reasons he didn't want to examine, the idea that Seraphina had another man waiting for her somewhere—that she wouldn't even mention that fact to him at any point when they talked—sent a streak of anger through Jehan's veins.

That she would look at him so wantonly the other night when this other male—what the fuck kind of name was Karsten, anyway?—obviously cared about her, needed her, made Jehan wonder if he'd read her wrong from the start.

Of course, she'd already confessed to him that she only agreed to participate in the handfast to collect a handsome payout at the end. So, why should it surprise him to realize she was already spoken for?

"You're breaking the rules." His voice was low and even, betraying none of the heat that was running through his veins.

She startled so sharply, the phone practically leapt out of her fingers. She scrambled to keep it and whirled around on the sofa to gape at him in horror.

"Jehan! I didn't hear you come in the room."

"You don't say." He gestured to the phone now clutched tight to her breast. "How'd you get that in here?"

She had the decency to look at least a little contrite. "I made Leila smuggle it in with the clothing she packed for me. She didn't want to, but I insisted. How was I supposed to go an entire week completely cut off from everything?"

"And *everyone?*" Jehan prompted. "Who's Karsten?"

Her face blanched. No need for her to ask him if he saw her texts. Her guilty look said it all. "He's my partner."

"Partner?" He practically snarled the word.

"My coworker. Karsten volunteers with me at the border camps."

Some of Jehan's irritation cooled at the explanation. "For a coworker, he sounds very eager to have you back. He's no good without you?"

Her expression relaxed into one of mild dismissal. "Karsten is...a bit dramatic. Right now, he's concerned about a food and medical supply shipment that's being held up at a checkpoint near Marrakesh. Normally

I make sure things clear without delays, but unfortunately this shipment didn't come in until after my parents called me home."

"What happens if the shipment doesn't get cleared?"

She crossed her arms over her breasts. "The food will rot and the medicine will spoil. It happens all too often."

"And this Karsten is unable to retrieve the supplies without you?" Jehan couldn't mask his judgment of the other man. If necessary food and medicine were sitting somewhere waiting to be delivered, he'd make damn sure it got where it needed to go.

Seraphina slipped off the sofa and walked to the marble-topped island where Jehan stood. "A lot of times, when things are delayed like this, my father's name helps loosen them up. Sometimes, it's a matter of finding the right palm to grease."

Jehan nodded. Corruption in local governments was nothing new. That Seraphina seemed comfortable navigating those tangled webs was impressive. She kept impressing him, and he wasn't sure he should like it as much as he did. "What do you think will free up this shipment of supplies?"

She shrugged faintly. "Does it matter? Karsten hasn't been able to get them on his own so far, and by the time our week is out here, it'll be too late. Food and medicine doesn't last long in the desert."

No, he supposed it didn't.

But maybe there was some way to fix the situation.

"You say you know the checkpoint where the supplies are being held up?"

"It's on the outskirts of Marrakesh. A lot of our materials pass through that same one."

Jehan considered. "That's only a few hours away from here by car."

"What are you saying?" She frowned. "Jehan, what are you thinking?"

"Let me borrow your phone."

She handed it over, still staring at him in question. Jehan entered his brother's number and waited for him to pick up. It took several rings, then Marcel's confused voice came over the line in greeting. "Hello?"

Jehan got right to the point. "I have a favor to ask of you."

"Jehan? What the hell are you doing calling me? And where did you get the phone? You know there's supposed to be no technology or outside communication—"

"I know," he bit off impatiently. "Where are you right now?"

"Ah...I'm home, but I'm getting ready to head out for a while. What's going on? Is everything all right with Seraphina?"

"She's fine. We're fine," Jehan assured him. "I need a vehicle. As soon as possible."

Marcel gasped. "What?"

Seraphina's eyes went about as wide as he imagined his brother's had just now.

"It's important, Marcel. You know I wouldn't ask if it wasn't."

"But you can't leave the villa. If you leave Seraphina alone out there, you'll be breaking the pact. Hell, you already are just by making this call to me."

"No one will know I called except you." Jehan glanced at Seraphina and shook his head. "As for breaking the pact by leaving her at the villa without me, not happening. She's coming with me, and we won't be gone long. No one will be the wiser."

"Except, once again, me." Marcel groaned. "I probably don't want to know what any of this is about, do I?"

"Probably not." Jehan smiled.

Marcel exhaled a curse. "Please tell me you don't want my Lambo."

"Actually, I was hoping for one of the Rovers from the Darkhaven fleet. With a full tank of fuel, if you would."

Marcel's deep sigh gusted over the line. "Does Seraphina realize yet what a demanding pain in the ass you can be?"

Jehan met her gaze and grinned. "I imagine she's figuring that out."

Marcel chuckled. "I'll drop it off at sundown."

CHAPTER 9

"Careful with that crate, Aleph. Those glass vials of vaccines are fragile."

Walking across the moonlit sand with her arm around one of the children from the refugee camp and a box of bandages held in her other hand, Sera directed another of the volunteers to the open back of the supply-laden Range Rover. "Massoud, take the large sack of rice to Fatima in the mess tent and ask her where she'd like us to store the rest of the raw grains. Let her know we have some crates of canned meats and boxes of fruit here too."

Behind her at the vehicle, Jehan was busy unloading the crates and boxes and sacks they'd just arrived with from the checkpoint near Marrakesh. Sera couldn't help pausing to watch him work. Dressed in jeans and a loose linen shirt with the sleeves rolled up past his *glyph-*covered forearms, he pitched in like the best of her other workers. Even better, in fact, since he was Breed. His strength and stamina outpaced half a dozen humans put together.

She still couldn't believe what he'd done for her tonight. For a village of displaced people he'd never met and didn't have to care about. All of the indignation and anger she'd felt toward him since their first night at the villa evaporated under her admiration for what he was doing now.

And it wasn't only admiration she felt when she looked at him.

There was attraction, to be sure. White-hot and magnetic.

But something stronger had begun to kindle inside her today. As unsettling as her desire for him was, this new emotion was even more terrifying. She *liked* him.

Jehan had intrigued her from their first introduction, even after she'd learned he made his living as a warrior. Their kiss at the banquet had ignited a need in her that she still hadn't been able to dismiss. And then, when he'd helped her out of her dress that initial night at the villa, she'd wanted him with an intensity that nearly overwhelmed her.

After he'd left her humiliated and awash in frustration, she'd almost been able to convince herself that he was simply an arrogant bastard and an aggravation she would just have to avoid or endure for the rest of their week together.

Now he had to go and do something kind for her like this. Something surprising and selfless.

Frowning, she turned away from him on a groan. "Come on, Yasmin. Let's go see if Fatima has anything good waiting in her kitchen tonight."

As they walked into the center of the camp, a Jeep was arriving from the other end of the makeshift village of tents and meager outbuildings. Yellow headlights bounced in the darkness as the vehicle jostled over the ruts in the dirt road into camp. The Jeep came to a halt several yards up and Karsten Hemmings hopped out of the driver's seat.

"Sera?" He jogged to meet her, a welcoming grin on his ruggedly handsome face. "I was down at the southern camp when I got word the supplies had been released." He gave her a quick kiss on the cheek as he took the box out of her hands. Then he reached down to pat the child's head with a smile. "What's going on? I thought you said you were going to be delayed with your parents for a few more days?"

She shrugged at the reminder of the small lie she'd told him. "I found an opportunity to get away for a little while, so I thought I'd run to Marrakesh and see what I could do about the supplies."

Karsten made a wry sound in his throat as he tossed the box of bandages to a passing camp volunteer. "How much did it cost this time?"

"A few thousand."

After haggling the checkpoint supervisor down as far as she could manage, she'd arranged to have the money wired to the corrupt official's personal account. It simply was the way business was done in her line of work sometimes, but all of the "few thousands" had added up over the years. Her account was nearly tapped dry now—at least until she completed the handfast and her father released her trust.

A group of children ran past and shouted for Yasmin to join them in a game of tag. The promise of treats in the mess tent quickly forgotten, the little girl ran off to join her friends.

"Stay close to camp, all of you!" Karsten called after them, watching them go. Then he cocked his head at Sera. "It's good to see you. When I heard you'd left to go to your family without telling anyone what it was about, I was afraid something was wrong." He glanced down, finally taking in her appearance. "What the hell happened to your clothes?"

Seeing how Leila had outfitted her for a week of lounging and potential romance, before Sera left the villa, she'd raided Jehan's wardrobe for something practical to wear out in the field.

She couldn't show up wearing any of the dresses or peasant skirts her sister had selected, so Sera had appropriated Jehan's white linen tunic from the night of the banquet and a loose-fitting pair of linen pants. With the pant legs rolled up several times, the waist held around her by a makeshift red silk belt, and a pair of her own kid leather flats, her clothing wasn't fashionable, but it was functional.

It also had the added benefit that it carried Jehan's deliciously spicy scent, which had been teasing her senses ever since she slipped the tunic over her head.

She wasn't sure how to explain what she was wearing, but then Karsten no longer seemed interested. His gaze flicked past Sera now, to where Jehan had just unloaded the last of the crates and supplies.

His brow rankled in confusion. "Who's that?"

"A friend," she said, unsure why she should feel awkward calling him that.

"He's Breed." Karsten's eyes came back to her now, wariness flattening his lips as he lowered his voice. "You brought one of them into the camp?"

Even though it had been twenty years and counting since the Breed were outed to mankind, prejudices still lingered. Even in her affable coworker, apparently.

"It's okay. Jehan is, ah...an old friend of my family." She waved her hand in dismissal of his concerns. "Besides, we won't be staying long. We have to get back to the villa tonight."

"The villa?"

Shit. She really didn't want to explain the whole awkward family pact and handfasting scenario to him. For one thing, it was none of Karsten's business—even if she did consider him a friend after they had dated briefly once upon a time. And maybe it was none of his business precisely *because* of the fact they had once dated.

Whatever the reason, she felt strangely protective of the time she'd spent with Jehan. It belonged to them—no one else.

"Once we get everything settled here in the camp, Jehan and I need to return. We're expected to be back as soon as possible." Which was about as close to the truth as she was going to get on that subject.

Karsten shook his head. "Well, you won't be leaving tonight. There's a big dust storm rolling in off the Sahara. It's moving fast, due here in the next hour or less. No way you'll be able to outrun it."

"Oh, no." A knot of anxiety tightened in her chest. "That's awful news."

"What's awful news?"

Jehan's deep voice awakened her nerve endings as sensually as a caress. He'd closed up the Rover and strode up behind her before she even realized it. When she pivoted to face him, she found his arresting blue eyes locked on Karsten.

"You must be Jehan." Instead of extending his hand in greeting, Karsten's fists balled on his hips. "I'm Karsten Hemmings, Sera's partner."

"Coworker." Jehan subtly corrected him. And as far as introductions went, his didn't exactly project friendliness either. His palm came down soft and warm—possessively—on her shoulder. "What's awful news?"

She tried to act as though his lingering touch was no big deal, as if it wasn't waking up every cell in her body and flooding her with heat. "There's a dust storm coming. Karsten says we may have to wait it out here at the camp. I know we need to get back soon, though. Your brother's waiting for us to return the Rover tonight—"

"Sera, if your friend has somewhere he needs to be," Karsten piped in helpfully, "then why don't you wait out the storm here at camp and I can bring you back to your parents' place tomorrow, after it passes?"

"Not happening." Jehan's curt reply allowed no argument. "If Seraphina stays for any reason, so do I."

Although he didn't say it outright, the message was broadcasted loud and clear. He wasn't about to leave her alone with Karsten, storm or no storm.

And if the protective, alpha tone of his voice hadn't sent her heart into a free fall in her breast, she might have found the good sense to be offended by his unprovoked, aggressive reaction to the only other male in her current orbit.

Karsten smiled mildly and lifted a shoulder. "Suit yourself, then. I'm going to start boarding things up ahead of the storm. If you need me, Sera, you know where I am."

She nodded and watched him walk away. Then she wheeled around to face Jehan. "You were very rude to my friend."

"Friend?" He snorted under his breath. "That human thinks he's more than a friend to you." Jehan's sharp blue eyes narrowed. "He was more than that at one time, wasn't he?"

"No." She shook her head. "We went on a few dates, nothing more. I wasn't interested in him."

"But he was interested in you. Still is."

"You sound jealous."

He exhaled harshly through flared nostrils. "Call it observant."

"I called it jealous." She stepped closer to him in the moonlight, weathering the heat that rolled off his big body and flashed from the depths of his smoldering gaze. His jaw was clamped hard, and the dark-stubbled skin that covered it seemed stretched too tightly across his handsome, perturbed face. "Why the hell should it bother you if Karsten is a friend of mine or something more? It's not like you have any claim on me. I could go after him right now and there's really nothing you can say about it."

A low sound rumbled from deep inside of him. "I would hope you don't intend to try me."

"Why? Because of some stupid pact?" Her voice climbed with her frustration. "You don't even believe in it, but yet you want to pretend we have to live by its terms."

"I don't give a fuck about the damned pact, Seraphina."

"That didn't stop you from using it as an excuse to make me feel like an idiot."

Sparks ignited in the shadowed pools of his eyes. "If you really think my walking away from you that night had anything to do with the pact, then you *are* an idiot."

She sucked in a breath, ready to hurl a curse at him, but he didn't give her the chance.

In less than a pace, he closed the distance between them. One strong hand slid into her loose hair and around her nape. The other splayed against her lower spine as he drew her to him and took her mouth in a blazing hot, hungry kiss.

Seraphina moaned as pleasure and need swamped her. Her breasts crushed against the firm, muscled slabs of his chest. Against her belly, his cock was a thick, solid ridge of heat and power and carnal demand. Hunger tore through her, quicksilver and molten. It burned away her anger, obliterated her outrage and frustration. As he deepened their kiss and his tongue breached her parted lips, all she knew was need.

She speared her fingers into his thick, soft waves and clung to him, lost in desire and oblivious of their surroundings. Willing to ignore everything so long as Jehan was holding her like this, kissing her as if he'd been longing for it as much as she had.

He drew back on a snarled curse and looked at her. His eyes snapped with embers, his pupils nothing but vertical slits in the middle of all that fire. His wet lips peeled back off his teeth and fangs as he drew in a deep breath, scenting her like the predatory being he truly was.

For a moment, she thought he was about to pick her up and carry her off to some secluded corner of the camp as if he owned her. She wouldn't have fought him. God, not even close.

But as they stood there, Sera felt a subtle sting start to needle her cheeks and forehead. Her eyes started to burn, then the next breath she took carried the grit of fine sand to the back of her throat.

The storm.

It was arriving even sooner than Karsten had warned.

She didn't have to tell Jehan. Pulling her close, he tucked her head against his chest and rushed with her toward the nearest outbuilding as the night began to fill with a roiling swell of yellow dust.

CHAPTER 10

By the time they reached the aluminum-roofed storage building several yards ahead, the biting wind had picked up with a howl. Sand churned across the camp, blowing as thick as a blizzard.

His body still charged with arousal, Jehan held Seraphina against him as he threw open the rickety wooden door. "Inside, quickly."

She no sooner entered the shelter than a muffled cry somewhere amid the storm drew both of them to full alert. The voice was small, distant. Unmistakably terrified.

"Yasmin." Seraphina's face blanched with worry. "Oh, God. The little girl who came to greet us when we arrived. She and some other children ran off to play a few minutes ago."

The cry came again, more plaintive now. There was pain in the child's voice too.

Jehan cursed. "Stay here. I'll find her."

Without waiting for her to argue, he dashed back into the night using the speed of his Breed genetics. The little girl's wails were a beacon through the blinding sea of flying sand. Jehan followed her cries to a deep ditch on the far side of the camp. At the bottom of the rugged drop, her small body lay curled in a tight ball.

"Yasmin?"

At the sound of her name, she lifted her head. Agony and terror flooded her tear-filled eyes. The poor child was shaking and sobbing, choking on the airborne sand.

Jehan jumped down into the ditch. Crouching low beside her, he sheltered her with his body as the sandstorm roiled all around them. "Are you hurt?"

Her dark head wobbled in a jerky nod. "My leg hurts. I was trying to hide from my friends, but I fell and they all ran away."

Jehan gingerly examined her. As soon as his palm skated over her left shin and ankle, he felt the hot pain of a compound fracture. The break streaked through his senses like a jagged bolt of lightning. "Come on, sweetheart. Let's get you out of here."

He collected Yasmin into his arms and carried her up from the ditch. At the crest of it, Seraphina was waiting. A heavy blanket covered her from head to toe as a makeshift shield from the storm. She opened her arms as Jehan strode toward her, enveloping him and the child as the three of them made their way across the camp.

"She needs a medic," he informed Seraphina as she murmured quiet reassurances to the scared child. "I felt two fractures in the lower part of the left fibula, and a fairly bad sprain in the ankle."

Seraphina's brows knitted for a second, then she acknowledged with a nod. "The medical building is in the center of camp. This way."

She set their course for one of the glowing yellow lights emanating through the sand and darkness up ahead.

Jehan didn't miss the uncertain glances he drew as he and Seraphina brought the injured child into the small field hospital. Their wariness didn't bother him. Being Breed, he was accustomed to the wide berth most humans tended to give him. And it didn't escape his notice that one of the nurses carrying a cooler with a large red cross on it made an immediate about-face retreat the instant her eyes landed on him—as if her stash of refrigerated red cells might provoke him to attack.

The humans needn't have worried about that. His kind only consumed fresh blood, taken from an open vein.

And right now, the only veins that interested him at all belonged to the beautiful woman standing next to him. Even dressed in his worn shirt and oversized pants, Seraphina stirred everything male in him the same way she stirred the vampire side of his nature.

Just because their kiss had been interrupted by the storm and a distressed child, that didn't mean he'd forgotten any of that fire Seraphina had ignited in him. Now that the little girl was safe and in the care of a doctor, Jehan's attention—all of his focus—was centered on how quickly he could get back to where he and Seraphina had left off.

But he stood by patiently as she made introductions and explained to her fellow volunteers that Jehan was her friend, that he was the one who went out into the storm to locate Yasmin. Seraphina's vouching for him seemed enough to put the humans at ease, since it was clear that everyone at the camp trusted and adored her.

He was beginning to feel likewise.

More than beginning to feel that way, in fact.

After the medic and nurses went back to their work, Seraphina turned to look up at him.

"When you brought Yasmin out of the storm, you said her leg was broken." He nodded, but that didn't seem to satisfy Seraphina's curiosity. "Actually, you said her fibula had two fractures and that her ankle was badly sprained. You were right, Jehan. According to the field medic just a few minutes ago, you were one hundred percent accurate. You told me you *felt* her injuries. You can feel physical injuries?"

He shrugged, barely acknowledging the ability he so seldom used.

"Can you heal them too?"

"No. And now you know my curse," he murmured wryly. "I can inventory someone's wounds, but I can't help them."

She tilted her head at him, warmth sparkling in her eyes. "You helped Yasmin tonight."

Jehan stared at her, unsure how to respond. Seraphina couldn't know how his so-called gift had hobbled him in his life. He'd grown up feeling useless, aimless. It wasn't until he'd found the Order that he realized there were other ways to do something meaningful with his life. That his life had purpose.

She was still studying him, looking gorgeous and far too interested in him as she held his gaze. "The storm's really blowing out there. Do you want to wait it out in here or would you rather go to my place?"

He arched a brow. "Your place?"

"My tent." She smiled, and the warmth of it went straight to his groin. "It's where I stay when I'm here at the camp for any length of time. It's not all that comfortable, but it is private."

Jehan's grin broke slowly across his face. "Miss Sanhaja, are you trying to seduce me?"

She licked her lips, tilting her head as she held his hungry gaze. "I think I might be."

Holy hell. The promise in her voice had his blood racing so hard and fast to his cock, he wasn't sure he'd make it to her tent.

"Lead the way," he drawled thickly, his fangs already punching out of his gums.

He held the blanket aloft over them as they dashed out of the medical building and raced through the blizzard of sand. Seraphina's tent stood toward the far end of the camp. By the time they reached it and found their way past the zipper and ties that secured the shelter's entrance, they were coated in a thin layer of grit. They stumbled inside together hand-in-hand, Seraphina laughing and breathless in the dark.

She left him for a moment, bending to turn on a lantern.

The soft light put a glow on her pinkened cheeks and on the flush of color rising up the smooth column of her throat, making the fine sand that dusted her skin glitter like diamonds. Under the windblown tangle of her long brown curls, her sandalwood-colored eyes were fathomless and filled with desire. Her breath was still racing and shallow, the outline of her breasts teasing him from under the crisp white linen of his shirt.

He'd never seen anything so lovely.

With the storm howling all around them, sand buffeting the tent like rain, Jehan stood speechless, the sight of her like this branding itself into his memory forever.

He couldn't resist reaching out to stroke the velvet of her cheek. And then that wasn't enough either, so he cupped her face in his hands and dragged her into a fierce kiss.

The instant their mouths met, it was as if no time had passed between their fevered kiss before the sandstorm and this electric moment now. Hell, it was as if they were merely picking up where they left off that first night at the villa. All of the hunger he felt for this female, all of the desire...it was right there below the surface, waiting for the chance to reignite.

And he knew that Seraphina felt it too.

On a moan, she melted against him, her lips parting to give his tongue the access it demanded. Heat licked through his veins at the taste of her passion, scorching everything in its path. In an instant, his fangs punched through his gums to fill his mouth. Need hammered in his temples, in his chest. In the aching length of his cock.

He groaned with the intensity of it.

He had to pace himself. Wanted to take this slowly with her, despite his own impatience to have her spread out beneath him as he buried himself inside her.

But Seraphina was merciless. Her wet mouth and gusting breath tore at his resolve. Her soft curves and strong, questing fingers on his shoulders and chest, in his hair, stripped away his already threadbare control.

Sliding his hands under the loose hem of the tunic, he greedily caressed the firm swell of her satin-covered breasts. Seraphina gasped, arching into him as he flicked open the front clasp of her bra and cupped her bare flesh in his palms. Her nipples were tight little buds that pebbled even harder as he rolled and tweaked them between his fingers, hungry to taste them.

He released her, but only so he could take the shirt off and feast on her with his eyes.

He drew the linen over her head and let it fall to the floor of the tent. The red sash holding up her pants came off next. He untied it and watched as the slackened waistband of the linen trousers slid off her hips to pool at her feet.

"So beautiful," he murmured, reaching out to run the backs of his knuckles down her arm, then across the flat plane of her belly. He ventured further, toying with the lacy edge of her delicate panties. "This is what I wanted to do that first night with you, Seraphina. Undress you inch by inch. Pretend I had the right to look at you like this and think I could ever be worthy of having you."

She slowly shook her head. "I don't want you to pretend, Jehan. Tonight, I don't want you to stop. I didn't want you to stop that first night either."

A sound escaped him, something raw and otherworldly. He slid his fingers into the scrap of fabric between her legs, and...holy fuck.

She was almost bare beneath the lace. And wet. So damn wet. Hot, liquid silk bathed his fingertips as he delved into her slick cleft.

She bit her lip, dropping her head back on a sigh. Holding on to him as he stroked her silky folds, she squirmed and shuddered against his touch. "Jehan, don't make me wait. Please, don't make me want like this again."

"No chance of that," he uttered, his voice like gravel in his throat, raw with desire. "Not tonight."

Not ever again, some possessive part of him growled in agreement.

He didn't know where it came from—the bone-deep sense that he belonged with this woman.

That she was *his*.

And that as ridiculous as the ancient pact between their families was, it had somehow delivered him to the one woman he craved more than any other before.

Jehan drew her mouth to his and kissed her again, as reverent as it was claiming. He broke contact only so he could strip out of his shirt and jeans, leaving both at his feet. He wore nothing underneath, and as soon as his cock sprang free, Seraphina's hands found him.

She stroked and caressed him, her fingers so sure and fevered, he nearly came on the spot.

Need twisted tight and hot with every slide of her hands over his stiff shaft, pressure coiling at the base of his spine.

Somehow, he managed to collect himself enough to douse the lantern with his mind. The tent plunged into darkness. Although the sandstorm raged outside, driving everyone in the camp indoors, he wasn't going to share Seraphina or this moment with anyone else.

Pulling her down onto the pallet of blankets and pillows with him, Jehan removed her panties, then smoothed his hand along every beautiful swell and delicately muscled plane on her nude body. The temptation of her sex was too much. The sweet scent of her arousal drenched his senses as he moved over her, parting her thighs until she was opened to him like an exotic flower.

One he couldn't wait to taste.

He lowered his head between her legs, groaning in a mix of agony and ecstasy as his tongue met her nectar-sweet, hot, wet flesh. His fangs were already fully extended, but at the first swallow of Seraphina's juices, the sharp points grew even larger.

The urge to bite—to draw blood and make her his in the most powerful way he knew how—rose up on him without warning.

No.

He tamped the impulse down hard, blindsided by the force of it.

Losing himself to carnal pleasure was one thing. Binding Seraphina to him for eternity was another. And it was a line he wouldn't cross.

He had no room in his life for a mate, and if she woke up in the morning with regrets, he sure as hell didn't want one of them to be irrevocable.

Tonight, he wanted to give her pleasure.

Selfishly, he wanted to give her the kind of pleasure that would ensure that every other male who'd ever touched her was obliterated from her memory.

Tonight, Seraphina was his—not because some ridiculous agreement said she should be, but because she wanted to be.

Because she felt the same undeniable desire that he did.

"Come for me," he rasped against her tender flesh. "I want to hear you, Seraphina."

"Oh God," she gasped in reply, arching up to meet his mouth as he kissed and sucked and teased with his lips and tongue. When she writhed and mewled in rising pleasure, he gave her more, sliding a finger through her juices and into the tight entrance of her body. She cried out as he added another, thrusting in tempo with his tongue's deep strokes.

He glanced up the length of her twisting body. "Open your eyes, beauty. I want to see you come for me."

She obeyed, lifting heavy lids, her gaze drunk with pleasure. "Jehan, please..."

Her hands tangled and fisted in his hair as he coaxed her higher, desperate for her pleasure—for her release—before he would let himself inside.

Ah, fuck. He'd never seen anything as erotic as Seraphina caught at the crest of orgasm. The sexy sounds she made. The unbridled response of her body. The tight, hot vise of her sheath, clamping down around his fingers as he flicked his tongue over her clit and drove her relentlessly toward a shattering release.

She held his gaze in the dark, and when she crashed apart a moment later, it was with his name on her lips.

Jehan couldn't curb his satisfied grin.

He rose over her, pressing her knees to her chest as he guided his cock between the slick folds of her sex. Her eyes were locked on his, her body still flushed and shuddering with the aftershocks of her release. He tested her tight entrance with a small thrust of his hips, groaning as her little muscular walls enveloped the head of his shaft.

He grasped for control and found he had none.

Not where this woman was concerned.

And why that didn't scare the hell out of him, he didn't know.

Right now, with Seraphina wet and ready for him, the question damn well didn't matter.

With a harsh curse, he flexed his pelvis and seated himself to the root.

CHAPTER 11

She gasped Jehan's name as he took her in one deep, breath-stealing thrust.

His wicked mouth and fingers had left her nerve endings vibrating and numb with sensation, her body slick and hot from release. But each rolling push of Jehan's hips stoked her arousal to life once more. His cock stretched her, filled her so completely she could barely accommodate all of his length and girth. She closed her eyes against the staggering ecstasy that built as he moved inside her, his powerful strokes and relentless tempo driving her to the edge of her sanity.

She'd never felt anything as intoxicating as the naked strength of Jehan's magnificent body. That all of his passion—all of his immense control—was concentrated on her pleasure was a drug she could easily become addicted to. Maybe she already was because her hunger for him was only growing more consuming with every hard crash of his body against hers.

Reaching up between them, he drew one of her legs down from where it lay bent against her chest and wrapped it around his waist as he shifted into an even more intense angle. The new position gave her access to his *glyph*-covered pecs and muscled abdomen, which she explored with questing fingers and scoring nails. She lifted her head and watched him pound into her, mesmerized by the violent, erotic beauty of their need.

Jehan made an approving noise in the back of his throat. "Do you like the way we look, Sera? Your legs spread open so wide for me, my cock buried in your heat?"

"Yes." *Oh, God.* Had she thought she was already at the brink of combusting? His dark voice inflamed her even more. She tore her gaze away from their joining only to meet the crackling fire that blazed down at her from his transformed eyes. "Jehan...I didn't know it could be like this. Watching you push inside me like you can't get deep enough. I love seeing us together like this. I love the way we feel."

"Mm," he responded, more growl than reply. "Then let me give you even more."

He set a new pace that destroyed her already slipping control. Another orgasm mounted and twisted inside her, sweeping her into a dizzying spiral of pleasure. She caught her lip between her teeth on a strangled moan as the climax swelled, nearing its breaking point.

Jehan's rhythm showed no mercy. He rode her harder, deeper, his hips pistoning furiously.

She arched beneath him, unable to hold on any longer. Turning her head into her pillow, she let go of a scream as her release broke over her in wave after wave of bliss.

Jehan pumped furiously as she came, then a rough curse ripped out of him. He tensed, his muscles hardening like granite beneath her fingertips as she clung to him. His amber-lit eyes blazed hot, locked on her.

He hissed her name, torment and pleasure etched in his handsome, savage face. Then a roar boiled past his teeth and fangs. His hips thrust viciously, then he plunged deep on a curse as the sudden, scorching flow of his seed erupted inside her.

She'd never felt so sated. So deliciously fucked.

She caressed Jehan as his body relaxed and his orgasm ebbed. But his cock had lost little of its stiffness inside her. And as he murmured rumbling praises for the way she felt, his strong fingers petting her hair and cheeks and breasts, that lingering stiffness had returned to steel again.

She couldn't control her body's response to him, nor could she curb her shaky sigh of pleasure as his shaft swelled to capacity and the walls of her sex clenched to hold him. She moved beneath him, creating a slick friction.

"Holy fuck, Sera." He closed his eyes for a moment, head tipped back on his shoulders as she invited him to take her again. When his gaze came back to hers, the fire that had been there before flared even hotter. "I should've walked away. Now, it's too late. It's too fucking late for both of us."

She nodded, knowing he was right. They should have resisted this heat that lived between them.

They should have refused the handfast and all that came with it.

They both should have realized that giving in to this desire would only spark a greater need.

For Sera, what she felt for Jehan went beyond physical need or even a passing affection. Tonight, she'd seen a new side of him. Not the arrogant Breed male who strode through life as if he owned the world. Not the Order warrior who dealt in ruthless justice and death.

Tonight, at the camp, she'd witnessed a different side of him. Jehan was a kind man, a compassionate man. She'd glimpsed the honor inside him, and now that she had seen those things, she would never be able to regard him in any lesser light.

So, yes. It was much too late for her to walk away from anything that happened between them tonight.

And if she should regret that fact, she never would.

Not when Jehan was looking at her the way he was now, with fever in his eyes and desire riding the furious arcs and swirls of his multicolored *dermaglyphs*. And not when his amazing cock was making her yearn to be taken all over again.

"On your knees this time," he commanded her, his deep voice husky and raw.

Her eyes widened in surprise, but she eagerly scrambled out from under him to obey. He loomed behind her, the heat of his presence scalding her backside. His fingers waded through their combined juices, wringing a desperate mewl from her throat as the wet sounds of his caresses joined the dry howl of the sandstorm still raging outside the tent.

She felt the thick length of his cock between her swollen folds. Then he grasped her hips in his hands and slowly impaled her on him, inch by glorious inch.

They set a less frantic pace now, somehow finding the will to savor the pleasure, making it last as long as they could hold out. After they had both climaxed again, they dropped into a lazy sprawl on her blanket-strewn pallet.

For a long while, there were no words between them. They lay together in the dark, listening to the hiss of swirling sand as the storm continued to sweep through the camp.

Sera was stretched alongside him, one arm resting on his chest. She traced the pattern of *glyphs* that spread over his smooth skin, memorizing the Breed skin markings that were unique to him alone. They were beautiful. And so was he.

"I need to thank you for tonight, Jehan."

He grunted. "No need, trust me." His strong arm tightened around her, bringing her closer against him. "I should be the one thanking you."

She rose up to look at his face. "No, I mean for what you did tonight. For helping me bring the supplies here. For going out into the storm to find Yasmin and make sure she got the care she needed for her injured leg."

He shrugged mildly. "Again, there's no need for thanks. I did what anyone would do."

"Not anyone," she said. "And I never would've expected it from you. I misjudged you when we met, and for that, I also owe you an apology."

He cupped her nape and brought her down to him for a tender kiss. "Maybe we both were too quick to judge. When you told me you only agreed to the handfast to collect the trust from your father, I assumed you were willing to take his bribe because you wanted the money for yourself. And not that it should matter why you wanted it, but it did. Tonight at the checkpoint, I know what you did. I realized what you've been doing all along—using your personal funds to buy clearance for camp supplies."

She frowned. "It's only money. How can I keep it when those supplies mean life or death to the people who depend on me?"

"Your work obviously means a lot to you." There was a soberness in his eyes as he studied her in the darkened tent. "You told me that night we walked in the garden that your work is a calling."

"I did say that, yes." It surprised her that he remembered the offhand remark.

"What did you mean, Seraphina?"

She glanced down at her hand where it rested on his chest. "When I was eighteen, I volunteered one winter at an orphanage about an hour away from our Darkhaven. My parents encouraged it, since I was orphaned as an infant too."

Jehan made an acknowledging sound. "A lot of Breedmates find their way into Breed households as abandoned and orphaned babies or young girls."

She nodded. She and her sister were both adopted by the Sanhajas in such a way. "I was lucky. Someone saw my birthmark and recognized that I was different. There was a place for me because of that. But there were no Breedmates in the orphanage I went to that year. Only human children. Many of them were refugees whose parents had been killed in wars or died of famine and disease." She curled her fingers into a tight ball. "There was so much pain in that place. I felt it every time I held a crying baby or embraced one of those sweet, terrified kids."

"You felt it," Jehan murmured, understanding fully now. He reached up to take her hand, bringing her knuckles to his lips. "You felt their emotional pain, because, like me, you're an empath."

Every Breedmate, like every Breed male, was born with a unique extrasensory ability. Some were blessings, others were less of a gift. Where Jehan could register physical injuries, hers was the ability to feel emotional pain with a touch.

"I thought I could handle it," she said. "But everything I felt stayed with me. Until my time working at the orphanage that winter, I didn't know how to help. Now I do what I can."

He'd gone quiet as she spoke, and Sera knew he understood. Given his own ability, Jehan probably understood her better than anyone else could.

"You're an incredible woman, Seraphina." He shook his head, his thumb stroking idly over her jawline. "I think I recognized that the minute we met, but I was too busy looking for reasons to dislike you. I wanted to find hidden flaws, since it was obvious I wasn't going to find any on the outside."

His praise warmed her. "I haven't been able to find much fault in you either. And believe me, I tried. I called you a killer when I found out you were a warrior with the Order. That wasn't fair. I know that now. I also thought your biggest personal flaw might be an overblown opinion of your own charms. I think you've proven the point tonight, though. I suppose I have to give credit where it's due."

He chuckled. "If what I just did with you was charming, then just wait until you see my wicked side."

She grinned down at him. "When can I look forward to that?"

"If you're not careful, sooner than you think."

He grabbed her ass and gave it a playful smack. Then he tumbled her onto her back and covered her with his hard, fully aroused body. The crackling embers in his eyes promised he was about to make good on his threat right then and there.

CHAPTER 12

The storm had passed some time ago.

Jehan lay on his back in the dark tent, holding Seraphina as she slept naked and draped over him in a boneless sprawl. He'd been awake for a while, listening to the calm outside and trying to convince himself that he needed to get out of bed.

As much as he hated to disturb her sleep or forfeit the pleasant feel of her resting sated in his arms, he knew he should go out and check their vehicle, make sure it wasn't buried under a mound of sand. With the weather cleared, he was eager to get on the road.

He guessed it to be early morning, probably only two or three hours after midnight. If they didn't delay too long, it was possible they could make it back to the villa before sunrise. Otherwise, it meant spending the day at the camp, waiting until sunset when it was safe for him to make the drive again.

And while he could think of a lot of interesting ways to pass the hours with Seraphina alone in her tent, he wasn't ashamed to admit that he'd rather explore those options in the comfort of the villa.

Which meant getting his ass out of her bed ASAP, so he could expedite that process.

With care not to wake her, he eased himself out from under her and rolled away from the thin mattress on the floor.

Dressing quietly, he then slipped out of the tent to begin the trek toward the place he'd parked the Rover. He was the only one outside so soon after the storm. He hoofed it through the quiet camp, his boots putting fresh tracks on the sand-drifted road that cut through the center of the tents and outbuildings.

The Rover could have been worse. Sand coated the black vehicle and had blown into every crack and crevice. He dug it out and brushed it down as best he could and was just about to start it up when his preternatural hearing picked up the sound of men's voices elsewhere in the dark. Somewhere near the main supply building.

Jehan recognized Karsten Hemmings's dramatic tenor instantly. The other man sounded like one of the helpers who'd assisted in unloading the delivery earlier tonight.

Jehan listened, suspicion prickling his senses. On instinct, he reached into the Rover and retrieved the pair of daggers he'd stored under the driver's seat. Although he had busted Seraphina's pretty ass over the fact she'd brought her phone to the handfast, his breach of the terms by bringing his Order patrol blades was probably the worst of the two offenses.

Right about now, he was damn glad he had the weapons.

Tucking one into his boot and the other into the back waistband of his jeans, he stole around the rear of the tents and outbuildings, his senses trained on the pair of men. Sand sifted with their quick footsteps. Karsten issued orders to his accomplice in a low, urgent whisper.

"Pick up the pace, Massoud! My contact has been waiting on this shit for days. We've got less than an hour to make the drop and collect our money."

What the hell?

Karsten's Jeep was parked at the rear of the outbuilding. The back hatch had been swung open, while Karsten and the other camp worker were apparently loading the vehicle with crates taken out of the main supply.

Jehan crept through the shadows, peering at the contents of the Jeep while both men had gone back inside the building for more. Three crates labeled as canned meat sat in the back of the vehicle. Supplies that he and Seraphina had delivered earlier tonight.

One of the crates had been pried apart, several of the cans inside opened. An odd blue glow emanated from inside the containers.

At first, Jehan wasn't sure what he was seeing.

Not canned meats, that much was certain.

Each container held a palm-sized electronic object comprised of a metal casing and a glass center chamber. Inside the glass was a milky blue substance that glowed like a vial of pure energy.

Like a source of harnessed, weapons-grade ultraviolet light.

Holy shit.

The instant realization dawned on him, Karsten's cohort came around the back of the building. He was empty-handed, but the second his eyes lit on Jehan, he reached for his gun and fired a panicked round. Reacting almost instantly, Jehan let his blade fly, dropping Massoud dead in the sand.

The discharged bullet flew wild into the air. The cracking report of the gunshot echoed, shattering the sleepy calm of the camp. Screams and commotion stirred at once in some of the nearby tents.

Karsten raced out of the supply building. "Massoud, for crissake—"

He drew up short when he came face to face with Jehan holding his comrade's gun.

Jehan bared his fangs. "Doing a little dealing on the side, I see. What's the going rate on UV grenades these days?"

Karsten narrowed his eyes. "More than you could imagine, vampire."

The impulse to blow the human's head off was nearly overwhelming. But caution warned him that this was also Seraphina's longtime coworker. She considered Karsten Hemmings her friend.

As much as Jehan wanted to waste the bastard for profiting off Breed-killing UV arms and using Seraphina's goodwill to front it, that call wasn't his to make. Not like this.

"We both know you're not going to use that gun on me," Karsten taunted. "She'll hate you for it. Of course, if you pull that trigger, you'd better be prepared to die with me."

It was then that Jehan noticed the human held something tight in his fist. The blue glow poured out between his fingers.

"The detonator is already tripped," he confirmed. "The UV blast won't give me more than a sunburn. You, however..."

Jehan ignored the threat. He would deal with the fallout if and when it occurred. Right now, he wanted answers. If he had any chance of getting information to the Order, he needed answers.

"Who's waiting for this shipment, Karsten? Who's paying you for this shit?"

"Oh, come now. I think you know. Every warrior in the Order should know the answer to that question." He chuckled. "Yes, I know you're one of them. I did some checking tonight. Made a few calls. You're part of the Rome unit."

Jehan glowered. "And you're part of Opus Nostrum."

Karsten pursed his lips and gave a faint shake of his head. "Merely a businessman. And a like-minded individual. I despise your entire race of blood-sucking monsters. If Opus wants your kind eradicated and a war to make it happen, I'm only too happy to help send you all to your graves. Or into the light, as the case may be."

"Karsten?" Seraphina emerged out of the darkness, disheveled and confused. "Oh, my God. Jehan, what on earth is going—"

"Seraphina, stay back!"

Jehan's warning came too late. She had already strayed right into the middle of the standoff.

And Karsten seized his chance to let his weapon loose.

The UV grenade went airborne.

Jehan had precious little time to react. He dived under the Jeep as the light exploded all around him. The power of it was immense. Even from beneath the undercarriage of the vehicle, he could feel the searing energy of the solar detonation. It extinguished a moment later, plunging the desert back into darkness.

He was shielded.

He was alive.

But the act of self-preservation had just cost him dearly.

He heard Seraphina cry out, and he knew Karsten Hemmings had her.

The realization tore his heart from his chest. He couldn't let her be harmed. He couldn't lose her.

He never wanted to lose her.

On a roar, Jehan rolled out to his feet to face the bastard. Karsten had a pistol on her, held against the back of her head. And Jehan had dropped his gun somewhere in the sand.

"Let her go."

Karsten sneered. "Let her go so you can have her? She deserves better than you, vampire. Better than anything you can ever give her."

Jehan wasn't going to argue when he was thinking the same thing now, miserable as he drank in the sight of her terrified face and her tender brown eyes pleading for him to help her.

"Let her go, Karsten. If you do, maybe I'll let you live. But only if Seraphina wants me to."

The human chuckled. "No, I don't think so. We're going to leave now. I'm going to make my drop and collect my money. Then Sera and I are going to get out of this godforsaken hellhole and enjoy our spoils." He nestled his open mouth against her cheek, the nose of the gun still pressed against her skull. "You'll see, my love. I can give you everything you need."

She winced and closed her eyes, a miserable sound curling up from her throat.

Jehan couldn't bear another second of her torment. He had to act. He had one chance to end this, but he couldn't do it without her total faith in him.

"Seraphina." He spoke her name softly, reverently. Hoping she could hear how much she meant to him. "Look at me, sweetheart."

Her eyes opened and found his gaze through the dark.

He couldn't say the words out loud without betraying his plan, but he needed her to understand. He needed her to trust him.

Do you trust me, Seraphina?

He said it with his eyes. With his heart.

Trust me, baby. Please...

She gave him a nearly imperceptible nod.

It was enough. It was all the permission he needed.

Moving with every ounce of Breed agility and speed he possessed, Jehan reached around to his back and pulled out the dagger he'd stashed there. He let it fly from his fingertips.

An instant later, Karsten Hemmings dropped to the ground, Jehan's blade protruding from the space between his wide-open eyes.

Jehan ran to Seraphina and pulled her into his arms.

In that moment, nothing else mattered.

Not Karsten Hemmings. Not the Jeep full of UV grenades, or Opus Nostrum.

Not even the Order mattered as he drew Seraphina close and kissed her with all the relief and emotion—all the love—he felt for her.

He stroked her beautiful face and stared down into the soft brown eyes that now owned his heart and his soul. "Come on," he said, drawing her under the protection of his arm. "Let's get out of here."

CHAPTER 13

Sera was still numb with shock and disbelief several hours later, after Jehan had driven them back to the villa.

Karsten's betrayal cut deep. That he had used her to free up the supplies containing his hidden cargo was bad enough. But the idea that greed and hatred had poisoned his humanity so much that he was willing to kill—willing to traffic in weaponry designed for the wholesale slaughter of the Breed—was unthinkable. It was unforgivable.

Countless innocent lives were saved today, now that the UV grenades had been diverted from their buyer and stowed safely inside the villa.

As for Karsten and Massoud, when the other camp workers and residents came upon the scene and heard what the two men had been up to, there had been no shortage of volunteers offering to dispose of their bodies in the desert so that Sera and Jehan could get on the road as quickly as possible to beat the sunrise.

Sera had considered Karsten a friend for years, but there wasn't any part of her that mourned his death today even for a second. If not for Jehan's quick thinking and speed with his blade, she had no doubt that Karsten would have killed her.

He had almost killed Jehan too.

The terror she'd felt at that possibility had nearly gutted her as she'd stood helplessly in Karsten's grasp. Even now, the reality of how close she'd come to losing Jehan left her physically and emotionally shaken.

But he was alive.

Because of his warrior skills, they both were alive.

"Are you all right, Sera?" His deep, caring voice wrapped around her as they stood inside the villa together. "Is there anything I can do for you?"

She shook her head but couldn't keep from moving into the shelter of his arms. This was all she needed. His warmth enveloping her. His strong heartbeat pounding steadily against her ear as she rested her head on his muscled chest. She just needed...him.

"You should call your brother," she murmured. Marcel had left two messages on her phone in the past couple of hours, asking them to contact him as soon as possible. "We should let him know we've returned, at least so he can stop worrying that we're going to break the pact."

Jehan's chest rumbled with a sound of disregard. "I should call the Order too, and tell them what I'll be bringing back to Rome with me in a few nights. But my brother and everyone else can wait. The only thing I'm concerned about right now is you."

He pulled back and looked at her, a dark storm brewing in the pale blue of his eyes. When he lifted her chin and took her mouth in a slow, savoring kiss, it was easy to imagine that what she saw in his gaze—what she felt in his embrace and in his tender kiss—was something deeper than concern or simple affection.

It was easy to imagine it might be love.

"You're trembling, Seraphina." He reached out to caress her face and shoulder. "And you're cold too. Come on. Let me take care of you."

Maybe Leila had been right—that there was some brand of magic at work when it came to the pact between their families. Sera could almost believe it now because with Jehan leading her through the villa, his fingers laced with hers, it was far too easy to imagine that everything they shared since entering the handfast was somehow paving a path toward a future together. A future that might just last an eternity.

She hadn't missed his reference to the life waiting for him at the end of the handfast. She couldn't pretend that her own life wasn't waiting for her too.

But for the next few nights, she wasn't going to let reality intrude.

Jehan brought her into the cavernous bathing room with its towering marble columns and steaming, spring-fed bath the size of a swimming pool. He sat her down on the edge, then crouched down in front of her to remove her shoes. The soft leather flats were caked with sand and spattered with Karsten's dried blood. Jehan hissed a low curse as he set them aside.

When he lifted his head to meet her gaze, there was doubt in his eyes. "Can you forgive me, Sera?"

"For saving me from Karsten?" She shook her head. "There's nothing to forgive."

"No." His mouth flattened into a grim line. "I mean, for saving myself. For giving him the chance to get a hold of you in the first place."

Oh, God. Is that what he thought? Is that what weighed on his conscience now?

Sera leaned forward to take his tormented, handsome face in her palms. His anguish was palpable. She could feel the dull pain of it through her empathic gift. "Jehan, when I saw that flash of light as Karsten let the grenade go, I knew it would be lethal to you. I thought I was about to watch you die. If you hadn't protected yourself, we both would've been dead today. You saved me."

He studied her for a long moment, as if he wanted to say something more. Then he turned his face into her hand and placed a kiss in its center before drawing out of her loose grasp. "Let's get these clothes off and get you warm."

He stood up, taking her with him. With careful hands, he undressed her, peeling off the rumpled linen tunic and her bra. Then he drew down the loose-fitting pants and her lacy panties beneath. His gaze drank her in slowly, his eyes crackling with amber sparks.

When he finally spoke, his voice was dark and gravelly, rough with desire. "Earlier tonight, when I saw you naked like this for the first time, I said you were beautiful."

She licked her lips. "I remember."

She would never forget anything he said in her tent a few hours ago, nor anything he'd done. Arousal spiraled through her, as much at the reminder as under the intensity of his gaze now.

"I said you were beautiful, Seraphina...but I was wrong." He cupped her cheek in his palm, then slowly let his fingers drift down her shoulder, his thumb pausing to caress the Breedmate mark on her upper arm. "You are exquisite. The loveliest female I have ever, and will ever, lay my unworthy eyes on."

She started to shake her head in protest of his self-deprecation, but his kiss caught her lips before she could speak.

All of her desire for him—all of her tangled emotions—rose up to engulf her. She wanted him.

Loved him so powerfully it staggered her.

Only fear held her confession back.

Fear, and need.

She pulled back, breath heaving. Wordlessly, she unbuttoned his shirt and pushed it off his strong arms. Each swirl and flourish of the *dermaglyphs* that tracked over his powerful chest and muscled abdomen was a temptation to her fingers and her mouth.

She touched and kissed and licked her way down his immense body, finally lowering herself to her knees before him. His lungs rasped with the ragged tempo of his breathing as she unzipped his jeans and slid them down his hard thighs.

His cock bobbed heavily in front of her, the thick shaft and blunt, glistening plum at the crown making her mouth water for a taste. He groaned as she grasped his length in her hands, his muscles tensing, breath hitching, as she stroked him from root to head and back again.

When she leaned forward and wrapped her lips around him, his spine arched and he let out a tight hiss and guttural snarl. She'd never held so much force and power in her hands before, nor in her mouth. She couldn't get enough. And as his body's response quickened, it only made her hungry for more. For all of him.

She glanced up as she sucked him and found his fiery eyes locked on her. His pupils were thin and wild, utterly Breed. His broad mouth was pulled into a grimace, baring his teeth and the enormous length of his fangs.

She moaned, overwhelmed by the preternatural beauty of the male staring down at her. His large palm cupped the back of her head, his long fingers speared into her hair as she took the full depth of him into her mouth at a relentless tempo.

"Seraphina," he uttered hoarsely. "Ah, fuck..."

On a sharp groan, he withdrew from between her lips and scooped her up into his arms as if she weighed nothing at all. He carried her down into the steaming bath, fastening his mouth on hers in an urgent, fevered kiss as he sank to his shoulders in the warm water with her held aloft in his arms.

He tore his mouth away from hers, scowling fiercely. "I'm supposed to be the one taking care of you, if you recall."

She lifted a brow in challenge. "Is that your charming side talking or your wicked one?"

Sparks flared in his hot gaze. "Which do you prefer?"

"I haven't decided yet." Pivoting under the surface of the water, she faced him on his lap and wrapped her legs around his waist. The thick jut of his cock rose tall between them, the crisp hair at its root tickling her sex. She looped her arms over his shoulders and drifted close for a teasing kiss. "Fortunately, we've got all day to figure it out."

His hands gripped her ass and he smirked against her mouth. "All day, and another five nights after that."

"You think it's long enough?" she murmured, her lips still brushing his.

His answering chuckle was purely male and totally wicked. As was the meaningful shift of his hips that positioned his erection at the hot and ready entrance of her body. "Why don't you tell me if it's long enough?"

He lifted her onto him, and her laugh melted into a pleasured sigh as he sheathed every last inch.

CHAPTER 14

When he'd first arrived at the villa, Jehan had imagined what Seraphina might look like unclothed and wreathed in the steam of the bathing room as he made love to her. Now he knew. And none of his fantasies were any match for the true thing.

She met his rhythm stroke for stroke. Arousal arced through him with each rotation of her hips, making his vision bleed red as fire filled his gaze. This woman had ruined him for any other. She destroyed him with a smile, with every moan and gasp, and he hadn't even begun to show her what true pleasure was.

He rocked inside her, balanced on the edge of madness for how incredible they felt together.

Eight nights wasn't enough.

The part of him that was more beast than man snapped at that tether. Eight nights was nothing. And they had already lost three of them.

The part of him that was nearly immortal demanded much more than that. It wanted forever.

Something he couldn't give Seraphina.

Not when forever meant one of them would have to give up the life that waited for them on the other side of the handfast.

Real life—the one that she had devoted herself to, and the opposite one he was equally committed to. Real life, where her selflessness had nearly gotten her killed a few hours ago, and where he was the Order warrior whose work revolved around violence and death. Where cowardly men like Karsten Hemmings served diabolical groups like Opus Nostrum.

He couldn't turn his back on the things that mattered to him any more than he could ask Seraphina to turn her back on hers.

But it was damned tempting to think about forever when they were enveloped within the fantasy of the handfast.

With his arms around her and her legs circling his waist as they moved together, joined beneath the fragrant, steaming water, forever was the only thing on his mind.

Eternity with Seraphina at his side.

As his Breedmate.

Bonded by blood.

The thought sent his gaze to the smooth column of her throat. Her pulse fluttered, beating with a rhythm he could feel echoing in his own veins. His fangs, already elongated from passion, now throbbed with an equally primal need.

A dangerous, selfish need.

One bite and there would be no other woman for him as long as he lived. All it would take was a single taste. Everything Breed in him pounded with the urge to sink his fangs into her flesh and take that binding sip.

Equally strong was his need to bind Seraphina to him by blood as well. If she drank from him, she would belong to no other male. His forever.

He couldn't do that to her.

He wouldn't.

Instead he guided her toward a fevered climax, driving into her body with all the hunger that rode him in his blood. He gave her pleasure, moving relentlessly until she broke apart in his arms on a scream.

Then he pivoted her around and moved in behind her to follow her over the edge.

As he came inside her on a shout, he couldn't dismiss the cold knowledge that the clock on their time together was ticking—so fast he could feel it in his bones.

Eight nights with Seraphina wasn't enough.

But somehow, at the end of it, he was going to have to find the strength to let her go.

CHAPTER 15

Sera woke from a long sleep later that morning feeling drowsy and sated. Sore in all the right places. She couldn't curb the smile that crept over her face as she recalled the hours she'd spent in the bathing room making love with Jehan. Their sex had been exhausting and incredible—which, she was beginning to realize, was the norm where he was concerned.

He was a tireless, wickedly creative lover. When she'd lost count of her orgasms and was sure she couldn't take any more pleasure, he had lifted her from the steaming pool and carried her to one of several nests of plump cushions and silk pillows on the floor for another bone-melting round.

If she'd thought watching their bodies move together in the darkness of her camp tent had been erotic, it had been nothing compared to seeing every carnal nuance of their passion in the candlelit reflection in the bathing room mirrors.

Just the thought of their tangled limbs and questing mouths had her pulse thrumming all over again as she wandered into the villa's kitchen for a light breakfast. Jehan was awake too—if he'd slept at all. His deep voice carried in a low, indistinct murmur from the main living area in the heart of the retreat. He was on her phone apparently. She hoped he had gotten back to Marcel after his brother's repeated messages for them to report in.

Sera made some tea and grabbed a peach from a bowl of fruit on the counter. Her long curls poured loose around her shoulders and over her bare breasts as she padded quietly out of the kitchen in just her panties to join him.

Biting into the ripe peach as she walked, she considered how much sweeter the juice would be if she were licking it off Jehan's muscled body. Or sucking it off the hard length of his cock.

Oh God...she had it bad for this male.

He made her feel more alive than anything in her life ever had. Yes, she lived for her work. It had fulfilled her for a long time, given her purpose. But Jehan gave her pleasure. He gave her yearning and contentment, excitement and peace. He had opened a part of her she hadn't even realized had been closed before.

Most unsettling of all, he made her long for the one thing she'd never imagined she might need. A mate by blood. A bond that could never be broken, not even by time.

As he'd made love to her hours ago, there had been a moment when she almost believed Jehan might want that too.

She wouldn't have refused him.

They'd been drunk with passion, and in the heat of that limitless pleasure, he could have taken all of her—body, heart, soul, and blood. She would have surrendered everything she was. Without even knowing what a future together might look like once the handfast was over and they left the cocoon of the villa.

She would give it all to him now too, clear-headed and sober.

Not at the end of their eight nights, but now.

And as much as it scared her, she had to let him know what he meant to her. Even more terrifying, she had to know if what she'd read in his tormented eyes a few hours ago was anything close to the depth of emotion she felt for him.

If he loved her too, then nothing else mattered. They would find a way to blend their lives and form their future together.

But as she rounded the corner of the corridor and overheard some of his conversation, all of her hopes faltered, then fell away. He wasn't talking to Marcel. She hung back, out of Jehan's sight as he spoke with one of his fellow warriors.

"I appreciate your understanding, Commander. I'm eager to be back in Rome to assemble my team and put the new mission into action. I'll be there as soon as my obligation here is over." He paused to listen to the warrior on the other end, then exhaled a heavy sigh. "No, I haven't made Seraphina aware of my decision. To be honest with you, sir, my mind is made up where she's concerned. I don't intend to give her any room to disagree."

He chuckled as if he and his comrade had just shared a joke.

Meanwhile, Sera felt as though she'd been punched in the gut.

He was going back to Rome. Eager to get back to his team there.

As for her, he'd just disregarded her as if she didn't matter to him at all.

Sickness roiled in her stomach, in her heart. She shivered, suddenly self-conscious of her nudity in the center of the romantic villa. Silently, she retreated back to the kitchen and dropped the half-eaten peach in the trash.

What a fool she'd been to let herself think this was anything more than a joke to him. It had been from the start. An obligation he felt compelled to fulfill.

One he just admitted to his commander that he would walk away from as soon as it ended.

Thank God she hadn't let herself look even more idiotic by confessing her feelings for him.

Now she had several more nights of torture to look forward to, knowing that Jehan couldn't wait to be finished with the handfast and leave her behind.

CHAPTER 16

Complaints of a headache had driven Seraphina outside to the sunshine for most of the afternoon. Jehan had tried to persuade her that another vigorous round of orgasms might make her feel better instead, but his attempt at humor—and seduction—had failed miserably.

If he wasn't mistaken, her escape to the daylight on the patio seemed no less deliberate now than it had that first full day they'd spent together at the villa. When she'd gone there in an effort to avoid his company.

Had he done something wrong?

Or had she realized how close he'd been to burying his fangs in her carotid the last time they'd made love and was now determined to steer clear of him?

Whatever it was, it bothered him that she didn't seem interested in talking to him about it.

Roaming around the villa alone while she avoided him outside was maddening. He missed her, and she had only been away from him for a couple of hours.

How empty would his life feel if she was gone from it for good?

That was the question that had ridden him most of the past twelve hours—ever since their escape from the danger at the camp. Now that he'd had Seraphina in his life, in his arms, how would he ever be able to return to his existence without her?

He thought he'd known the answer, but maybe he was mistaken.

As twilight fell outside and she still didn't come inside to face him, Jehan decided he had to know. If she didn't feel the way he did, then he was ready to call off the rest of the handfast and try to save some shred of his sanity, if not his dignity.

He was stalking toward the patio doors when a knock sounded on the villa's front entrance.

Diverted from his mission, Jehan swung around and went over to see who it was.

Marcel stood there in the moonlight, grinning like an idiot.

And beside him—clinging to his arm with an equally besotted smile on her face—was Leila.

"You didn't return my call, brother."

Jehan raked a hand through his mussed hair and blew out an impatient curse. "Yeah. I, ah, was just about to do that."

"Bullshit." Marcel gestured to the Range Rover. "What the hell happened to the Rover? It looks like you drove it through a sand dune."

"Long story," Jehan said. "Suffice it to say things have been somewhat...interesting around here."

"Things have been a bit interesting with me too. With us." Marcel glanced at Leila, and she bit her lower lip as if to stifle the giggle that burst out of her anyway.

Jehan glanced at both of them. "What the hell are you talking about?"

Leila tried to peer around him, into the villa. "Where's Seraphina?"

"She's out on the patio, getting some air. Why are the two of you grinning like you've lost your damn minds?"

"We're in love!" Leila exclaimed.

"And we're blood-bonded," Marcel added.

"What?" Before Jehan could choke out his astonished response, Seraphina did it first. She stood behind him now in a long skirt and curve-hugging tank, a look of utter shock on her face. She crossed her arms. "What do you mean you're in love? How did that happen? And blood-bonded so soon? For God's sake, you only just met each other."

Jehan glanced at her, tempted to point out that they'd only just met too and he was already ruined for anyone else. But her pained expression kept him silent.

Marcel and Leila's excitement left no time for him to reply either. The pair stepped inside, practically vibrating with their news.

"We've been spending a lot of time together the past several days," Leila gushed.

Marcel wagged his brows at her. "And a couple of nights."

"Marcel!" She rolled her eyes, but her cheeks were flooded with bright color. "At first, we thought we only had the handfast in common.

We both wanted it to be a success, of course. And honestly, we thought the two of you would make an adorable couple."

Jehan noted a cooler shift in Seraphina's posture as her sister mentioned the handfast. "How can you be sure you're not making a terrible mistake, Leila? You don't know anything about him. No offense, Marcel. You do seem like a good, decent male."

Unlike his brother? Jehan wondered.

Leila stared up at Marcel, warmth beaming from her eyes. "He makes me feel alive, Sera. He makes me laugh. He makes me feel special and beautiful, like I'm the only woman he sees."

Marcel cupped her face in a tender caress. "Because you are."

They kissed, leaving Jehan in awkward silence next to Seraphina. He glanced at her, but she stared rigidly ahead, refusing to meet his gaze.

"Congratulations," she murmured as the jubilant couple finally stopped devouring each other's faces. "I'm happy for you both. I'm sure our families will be happy to hear this news too."

"That's why we're here," Marcel said. "The handfast—"

Leila nodded. "Now that Marcel and I are blood-bonded, there's no need to continue with the handfast. It's over as of right now."

Marcel must have read Jehan's grim expression. He cleared his throat. "That is, unless you *want* to continue...?"

"Don't be ridiculous," Seraphina replied quickly. "Neither one of us wants that. We're both very eager to be done with this obligation and get back to our real lives. Isn't that right, Jehan?"

He scowled, uncertain how to answer. It seemed obvious that continuing the handfast with him wasn't what she wanted. He was impatient to get on with his life outside the villa too, but only if she would be part of it.

She stared at him as he struggled with the urge to tell her how he felt and risk her rejection in front of both their oblivious, elated siblings.

"Sera," he murmured.

But she was already pivoting away from him. "Now that this farce is over, I'll go collect my things."

When she sailed off in a hurry, both Marcel and Leila gaped at him.

"What the hell did you do to her, brother?"

Jehan shook his head. "I don't know." And then, the truth settled over him. Something about what she said. Something about *how* she said it...

She'd heard him today.

His conversation with Lazaro Archer back in Rome.

He cursed under his breath. Then he started to chuckle.

Marcel frowned at him. "She's pissed as hell at you about something and you're laughing?"

"Yeah, I am." Because now he understood her cold-shoulder today. He understood her anger at him now. And he'd never felt more elated about anything in his life.

Rounding up his brother and Leila, Jehan pushed both of them out the door.

"What are you doing?"

"Sending you on your way," he replied. "Don't come back for four more nights. This handfast isn't over until I say it is."

He closed the door on their confused faces, then turned to go after his Breedmate.

CHAPTER 17

Sera folded the red silk gown and placed it on the bed, trying not to let her heart crumble into pieces.

Outside the massive bedroom suite, the villa had gone quiet. As much as she wanted to celebrate Leila and Marcel's newfound love and bond, part of her was aching for everything she thought she might have had with Jehan.

Now that the handfast was over, she didn't even have those few remaining nights left with him.

Which was probably for the best.

Being around him now was its own kind of torture.

He was already making plans without her. Plans he didn't intend to discuss with or allow her any say in.

So why should she mourn the fact that their week together had just been cut short?

"Where do you think you're going?"

She froze at the sound of his voice but forced herself not to turn around. If she did, she was afraid she'd be tempted to run to him. With her heart so heavy in her breast, she was afraid she'd be unable to keep herself from whirling on him with pounding fists and streaming tears. Demanding that he explain how he could look at her so tenderly and make love to her so possessively if he only meant to leave her behind in a few more nights.

Although she didn't hear him move, she felt the heat of his large body at her spine. "I asked where you think you're going, Seraphina."

"Home," she said. "As soon as possible, I hope."

She walked back into the wardrobe to retrieve another of the pretty, feminine dresses that Leila had packed for her. Jehan was waiting when she came out. He had placed her bag on the floor, and now he sat on the edge of the bed, his sky blue eyes holding her in an unwavering stare.

Why did he have to look so intense and imposing, so impossible to ignore?

The sight of him waiting there, his handsome face grim with purpose, made her limping heart start to gallop.

She forced herself to move, walking over to pick up her bag and place it on a nearby chair so she could continue filling it. "Shouldn't you be packing your things too? If we're lucky, we might be able to get out of here in the next hour or so."

"I'm not leaving, Seraphina."

She glanced up at that. She couldn't help herself.

He stood up and walked over to her. "I'm not going anywhere tonight. Neither are you."

"What are you talking about?"

Her breath caught as he closed the space between them. As always, his presence seemed to suck all of the air out of the room. Right now, it was leeching away some of the resolve she wanted to hold on to so desperately.

"You heard it yourself, Jehan. The handfast is over. We've both made good on our obligations to our families, so now we're free to go."

He shook his head, his expression sober. "Eight nights, Sera. That's what we agreed to. I'm holding you to it. I don't give a damn if the pact terms say you can leave me now. I have four nights left with you, and I mean to claim them." He reached out and stroked his fingers down the side of her face. "I mean to claim *you*, Seraphina. As my woman. As my Breedmate."

"What?" Shock and confusion washed over her. "But I heard you on the phone today. You said you were leaving. That you had decided to go back to Rome. You disregarded me to your commander as if I didn't matter at all. I heard you—"

His thumb swept over her lips, stilling them. "What you apparently didn't hear was that I also told Lazaro Archer I had fallen in love with you."

No, she hadn't heard that.

And hearing it now sent spirals of joy and relief twisting through every cell in her body.

"You didn't hear me tell him that I needed to make a place for you in my life. Or that I couldn't leave the handfast without knowing you were mine." He caressed her cheek, eyes smoldering with affection and desire. "My life is with the Order, Sera. I can't give that up."

"I would never ask that of you, Jehan. I understand that you're doing something important, something that you're devoted to. After what we found at the camp, I realize your mission with the Order has probably never been more crucial."

"No, it hasn't," he said. "I can't leave my duty, but I know you can't give up yours either. I'm not going to ask you to leave your life behind to be with me in Rome."

She frowned, grateful that he understood what her work meant to her, yet unsure how their two worlds could mesh as a mated couple.

"That's why I've decided to pull a new team together here in Morocco. After last night, it's obvious that Opus has a strong presence here, so I've been tasked with pursuing those leads here on African soil. I'll work out the details with Commander Archer when I return to Rome at the end of the week."

She couldn't believe what she was hearing. She couldn't believe what he was doing for her. For them both. For the new bond he meant for them to share.

"Jehan, I don't know what to say."

He lifted her chin on the edge of his fingers. "You can start by saying you love me."

"Yes," she whispered. Then she said it again with all the elation in her soaring heart. "I love you."

He drew her close and kissed her, his lips brushing hers with such tenderness she wanted to weep. The next thing she knew, he had her spread beneath him on the bed. As he undressed her, then hurriedly stripped off his own clothing, his *dermaglyphs* pulsed with all the deep colors of his desire. His cock stood erect and enticing, awakening a powerful hunger in her—for his body, and for his blood.

Jehan clearly knew what she was feeling. His own hungers blazed in his transformed eyes and in every formidable inch of his naked flesh.

His fiery gaze scorched her face as he looked at her in utter devotion.

And need.

So much need, it rocked her.

He lowered himself between her legs and entered her slowly, as he bent to lick a searing path along her jawline, then her neck. "You're mine, Sera."

"Yes," she gasped, arching into his abrading kiss as his fangs tested the tender flesh of her throat. "For the next four nights, I'm yours however you want me, Jehan."

He glanced up at her, baring those beautiful, sharp tips with his hungry, definitely wicked smile. He gave a slow shake of his head. "Four more nights is only the beginning. Starting now, you're mine forever."

She nodded, too swept up in love and desire to form words.

Emotion overwhelmed her as she watched him bite into his wrist to open his veins for her. "Drink from me," he rasped thickly, bringing the punctures to her parted lips.

Sera fastened her mouth to the wounds and stroked her tongue across the strong tendons of his wrist. His blood called to her, more deeply than she could ever have imagined. She moaned as the first swallow roared through her senses, into her cells. She drank more, reveling in the power of the bond as Jehan's essence—his life—became part of hers.

And all the while she drank, he rocked within her, creating a pleasure so immense she could hardly bear it.

"You're mine, Seraphina." He stared down at her as she fed, as she came on a shattered scream. "Starting tonight, you're only mine."

"Yes."

On a rumble of satisfaction, he drew his wrist to his mouth and sealed the punctures closed with a swipe of his tongue. His blazing eyes were locked on her throat.

Sera brought her arms up around him as he lowered his head to her carotid and licked the fluttering pulse point that beat only for him.

And when her handsome Breed warrior—her eternal love—sank his fangs into her vein and took his first sip, Seraphina smiled.

Because whether she believed in magic or not, tonight she was holding the prince, the fairy tale, and the happily ever after in her arms.

Sign up for the 1001 Dark Nights Newsletter
and be entered to win a Tiffany Key necklace.

There's a contest every month!

Go to www.1001DarkNights.com to subscribe.

As a bonus, all subscribers will receive a free
1001 Dark Nights story
The First Night
by Lexi Blake & M.J. Rose

Turn the page for a full list of the
1001 Dark Nights fabulous novellas...

1001 Dark Nights

WICKED WOLF by Carrie Ann Ryan
A Redwood Pack Novella

WHEN IRISH EYES ARE HAUNTING by Heather Graham
A Krewe of Hunters Novella

EASY WITH YOU by Kristen Proby
A With Me In Seattle Novella

MASTER OF FREEDOM by Cherise Sinclair
A Mountain Masters Novella

CARESS OF PLEASURE by Julie Kenner
A Dark Pleasures Novella

ADORED by Lexi Blake
A Masters and Mercenaries Novella

HADES by Larissa Ione
A Demonica Novella

RAVAGED by Elisabeth Naughton
An Eternal Guardians Novella

DREAM OF YOU by Jennifer L. Armentrout
A Wait For You Novella

STRIPPED DOWN by Lorelei James
A Blacktop Cowboys ® Novella

RAGE/KILLIAN by Alexandra Ivy/Laura Wright
Bayou Heat Novellas

DRAGON KING by Donna Grant
A Dark Kings Novella

PURE WICKED by Shayla Black
A Wicked Lovers Novella

HARD AS STEEL by Laura Kaye
A Hard Ink/Raven Riders Crossover

STROKE OF MIDNIGHT by Lara Adrian
A Midnight Breed Novella

ALL HALLOWS EVE by Heather Graham
A Krewe of Hunters Novella

KISS THE FLAME by Christopher Rice
A Desire Exchange Novella

DARING HER LOVE by Melissa Foster
A Bradens Novella

TEASED by Rebecca Zanetti
A Dark Protectors Novella

THE PROMISE OF SURRENDER by Liliana Hart
A MacKenzie Family Novella

FOREVER WICKED by Shayla Black
A Wicked Lovers Novella

CRIMSON TWILIGHT by Heather Graham
A Krewe of Hunters Novella

CAPTURED IN SURRENDER by Liliana Hart
A MacKenzie Family Novella

SILENT BITE: A SCANGUARDS WEDDING by Tina Folsom
A Scanguards Vampire Novella

DUNGEON GAMES by Lexi Blake
A Masters and Mercenaries Novella

AZAGOTH by Larissa Ione
A Demonica Novella

NEED YOU NOW by Lisa Renee Jones
A Shattered Promises Series Prelude

SHOW ME, BABY by Cherise Sinclair
A Masters of the Shadowlands Novella

ROPED IN by Lorelei James
A Blacktop Cowboys ® Novella

TEMPTED BY MIDNIGHT by Lara Adrian
A Midnight Breed Novella

THE FLAME by Christopher Rice
A Desire Exchange Novella

CARESS OF DARKNESS by Julie Kenner
A Dark Pleasures Novella

Also from Evil Eye Concepts:

TAME ME by J. Kenner
A Stark International Novella

THE SURRENDER GATE By Christopher Rice
A Desire Exchange Novel

SERVICING THE TARGET By Cherise Sinclair
A Masters of the Shadowlands Novel

Bundles:

BUNDLE ONE

Includes:

Forever Wicked by Shayla Black

Crimson Twilight by Heather Graham

Captured in Surrender by Liliana Hart

Silent Bite by Tina Folsom

BUNDLE TWO

Includes:

Dungeon Games by Lexi Blake

Azagoth by Larissa Ione

Need You Now by Lisa Renee Jones

Show My, Baby by Cherise Sinclair

BUNDLE THREE

Includes:

Roped In by Lorelei James

Tempted By Midnight by Lara Adrian

The Flame by Christopher Rice

Caress of Darkness by Julie Kenner

About Lara Adrian

LARA ADRIAN is the *New York Times* and #1 internationally best-selling author of the Midnight Breed vampire romance series, with nearly 4 million books in print and digital worldwide and translations licensed to more than 20 countries. Her books regularly appear in the top spots of all the major bestseller lists including the *New York Times*, *USA Today*, *Publishers Weekly*, Indiebound, Amazon.com, Barnes & Noble, etc.

Lara Adrian's debut title, Kiss of Midnight, was named Borders Books best-selling debut romance of 2007. Later that year, her third title, Midnight Awakening, was named one of Amazon.com's Top Ten Romances of the Year. Reviewers have called Lara's books "addictively readable" (Chicago Tribune), "extraordinary" (Fresh Fiction), and "one of the best vampire series on the market" (Romantic Times).

With an ancestry stretching back to the Mayflower and the court of King Henry VIII, Lara Adrian lives with her husband in New England, surrounded by centuries-old graveyards, hip urban comforts, and the endless inspiration of the broody Atlantic Ocean.

Connect with Lara online:

Website: http://www.laraadrian.com/
Facebook: https://www.facebook.com/LaraAdrianBooks
Twitter: https://twitter.com/lara_adrian
Pinterest: http://www.pinterest.com/laraadrian/

Don't miss the newest novel in the New York Times best-selling Midnight Breed series by Lara Adrian!

BOUND TO DARKNESS
On sale now in eBook, print and audiobook

Chapter 1

Titanium spikes slashed the fighter's face, spraying blood across the floor of the steel cage and thrilling the crowd of cheering spectators inside the underground fighting arena. Gritty industrial music pounded from the dance club upstairs, bringing the din to a deafening pitch as the long match between the pair of Breed males built toward its finish.

Carys Chase stood near the front, among the throng of avid spectators as Rune's fist connected with his opponent's face again. More shouts and applause erupted for the undefeated champion of Boston's most brutal arena.

The fights were technically illegal, but highly lucrative. And since the outing of the Breed to their terrified human neighbors twenty years ago, there were few sporting events more popular than the outlawed gladiator-style matches pitting a pair of six-and-a-half foot, three-hundred pound vampires against each other in a closed, steel mesh cage.

Blood was essential to Carys and her race, but sometimes it seemed mankind was even more thirsty for it. Especially when the spillage was restricted to members of the Breed.

Although even Carys had to admit that watching a vampire like Rune fight was a thing of beauty. He was dangerous grace and lethal savagery.

And he was hers.

For the past seven weeks—since the night she'd stepped into La Notte with a small group of friends and first saw Rune battling inside the cage—they had been practically inseparable. She had fallen fast and hard and deep, and hadn't looked back for a second.

Much to her parents' dismay. They and her twin brother, Aric, had all but forbade her to see Rune, basing their judgment on his profession and reputation alone. They didn't know him. They didn't want to know him either, and that hurt. It pissed her off.

Which is why, with a full head of steam and a stubborn streak inherited from both of her parents, Carys had recently moved out of the Chase family Darkhaven and in with her best friend, Jordana Gates.

Leaving home to get her own place hadn't gone over well, particularly with her father, Sterling Chase. As the commander of the Order's presence in Boston, he, along with the Order's founder, Lucan Thorne, and the other district commanders, were the de facto keepers of the peace between the Breed and mankind. No easy task in good times, let alone the precarious ones they lived in now.

Carys understood her father's concern for her safety and wellbeing. She only wished he could understand that she was a grown woman with her own life to lead.

Even if that life included a Breed male who chose to make his living in the arena.

All around her now, the spectators chanted their champion's name. "Rune! Rune! Rune!"

Carys joined in, awed by his domination of the fighting ring even as the woman in her cringed every time fists smashed on flesh and bone, regardless of who was on the receiving end. And she could admit, at least to herself, that being in love with him had made her hope for the day he might decide to climb out of the cage for good.

No one had ever beaten Rune—and more than a few had died trying.

He prowled the cage with fluid motion, naked except for the arena uniform of brown leather breeches and fingerless gloves bristling with titanium spikes. The sharp metal ensured every blow was a spectacle of shredding flesh and breaking bone for the pleasure of the crowd.

Also crafted primarily for the entertainment of the sport's patrons was the U-shaped steel torc around the fighters' necks. Each combatant had the option of hitting a mercy button inside the cage, which would deliver a debilitating jolt of electricity to his opponent's collar, halting the match to afford the weaker fighter a chance to recover before resuming the bout.

Although Rune had been the recipient of countless juicings when he climbed into the ring, he had never stooped to using the mercy button.

Neither did his opponent tonight. Jagger was one of La Notte's crowd favorites too, a black Breed male whose own record of wins was almost as impressive as Rune's. The two fighters were friendly outside the arena, but no one would know it to see them now.

Being Breed, Jagger healed from his injuries in seconds. He wheeled on Rune with a deafening roar, plowing forward like a bull on the charge. The contact drove Rune back against the cage. Steel bars groaned, straining under the sudden impact of so much muscle and might. The spectators directly below shrieked and shrank away, but the fight had already moved on.

Now it was Rune on the offense, tossing Jagger's massive body across the cage.

Game or not, the clash of fists and fangs brought out the savage in just about any Breed male. Jagger got to his feet, his lips peeled back from his sharp teeth on a furious sneer. His *dermaglyphs* pulsed with violent colors on his dark skin. He rounded on Rune, amber fire blazing from his eyes as he crouched low and prepared to make another bruising charge.

Opposite him in the cage, Rune stood tall, his massive arms at his sides, his stance deceptively relaxed as he and Jagger circled each other.

Rune's Breed skin markings churned with raging colors too. His midnight-blue eyes crackled with hot sparks as he studied his opponent. Rune's fangs were enormous, razor-sharp tips gleaming in the dim lights of the arena. But beneath the sweat-dampened fall of his dark brown hair, his rugged, granite-hewn face was an utter, deadly calm.

This was Rune at his most dangerous.

Carys's breath stilled as Jagger leapt, catapulting and cartwheeling in a blur of furious motion across the ring. One foot came up at Rune's face like powerful hammer, so fast, Carys could hardly track its motion.

But Rune had. He grabbed Jagger's ankle and twisted, dropping the fighter to the floor. Jagger recovered in less than an instant, pivoting on his elbow and sweeping Rune's legs out from under him with another smooth kick.

The move was swift and elegant, but it opened Jagger up for sudden defeat.

Rune went down, but took Jagger with him, tackling him into an impossible hold on the floor of the cage. Jagger struggled to break loose, but Rune's spiked knuckles kept the fighter subdued.

Howls and applause thundered through the arena as the clock counted down on the end of the match, with Rune about to claim yet another win.

As Carys cheered his certain victory, she felt a prickle of awareness on the back of her neck. She glanced behind her toward the back of the club. Two of her father's Breed warriors had just come inside.

Shit.

Dressed in the Order's black fatigues, Jax and Eli scanned the massive crowd, ignoring the spectacle inside the cage as they sought to locate her. She was getting used to seeing the Order's babysitting patrol every night, but that didn't make it any less annoying.

Maybe her father's patience had finally reached its end. She knew him well enough not to put it past him to send his warriors out to collect her and eventually bring her home. By force if needed.

Ha. Let them try.

As one of the rare few females of the Breed *and* a daywalker, Carys was every bit as strong as any male of her kind. Stronger than most, given that her mother, Tavia Chase, was a laboratory-created miracle comprised of half-Ancient and half-Breedmate genetics.

But she didn't need to resort to physical strength to avoid Jax and Eli. Carys had another ability at her disposal—this one inherited from her father.

As she stood among the crowd near the front of the arena, Carys quieted her mind and focused on her surroundings. Gathering and bending the shadows around her, she concealed herself in plain sight. No one would see her so long as she held the shadows close.

She waited, watching the pair of Order warriors stroll deeper into the club to scan the hundreds of humans and Breed packed inside. Carys drifted deeper into the throng, unseen by anyone. Jax and Eli gave up after a few minutes of searching. Carys smiled from within her magic as she watched them finally leave.

Meanwhile, the match in the cage was over. Rune and Jagger had taken off their metal torcs and gloves. They clapped each other on the shoulder, both mopping the blood and sweat from their faces as the announcer declared the winner.

Carys let her shadows fall away then. The hatch on the cage opened to let out the combatants. She raced to meet Rune, shouting his name and applauding with the rest of the throng as her man collected yet another victory.

Rune's rugged face lit up with private promise when he saw her. The brutal, fearsome fighter stepped out of the cage and caught her around the waist, hauling her to him.

His dark eyes glittered with need he didn't even try to conceal. Ignoring the cheers and applause that swelled around him, he took her mouth in a possessive kiss.

Then he scooped her up and carried her out of the arena.

Welcome to Storm, Texas, where passion runs hot, desire runs deep,
and secrets have the power to destroy...

Nestled among rolling hills and painted with vibrant wildflowers, the bucolic town of Storm, Texas, seems like nothing short of perfection.

But there are secrets beneath the facade. Dark secrets. Powerful secrets. The kind that can destroy lives and tear families apart. The kind that can cut through a town like a tempest, leaving jealousy and destruction in its wake, along with shattered hopes and broken dreams. All it takes is one little thing to shatter that polish.

Reading like an on-going drama in the tradition of classic day and night-time soap operas like Dallas, Dynasty, and All My Children, *Rising Storm* is full of scandal, deceit, romance, passion, and secrets.

With 1001 Dark Nights as the "producer," Julie Kenner and Dee Davis use a television model with each week building on the last to create a storyline that fulfills the promise of a drama-filled soap opera. Joining Kenner and Davis in the "writer's room" is an incredible group of *New York Times* bestselling authors such as Lexi Blake, Elisabeth Naughton, Jennifer Probst, Larissa Ione, Rebecca Zanetti and Lisa Mondello who have brought their vision of Storm to life.

A serial soap opera containing eight episodes in season one, the season premiere of Rising Storm, TEMPEST RISING, debuts September 24th with each subsequent episode releasing consecutively this fall.

So get ready. The storm is coming.

Experience Rising Storm Here... http://risingstormbooks.com

On behalf of 1001 Dark Nights,

Liz Berry and M.J. Rose would like to thank ~

Steve Berry
Doug Scofield
Kim Guidroz
Jillian Stein
InkSlinger PR
Dan Slater
Asha Hossain
Chris Graham
Pamela Jamison
Jessica Johns
Dylan Stockton
Richard Blake
BookTrib After Dark
The Dinner Party Show
and Simon Lipskar

Made in the USA
Middletown, DE
14 December 2015